THE
BAKER'S
LEGACY

THE BAKER'S LEGACY
SEQUEL TO *THE BAKER'S DAUGHTER*

D. P. CORNELIUS
DEIRDRE LOCKHART, EDITOR

Columbus, Ohio

This book is a work of fiction. The names, characters and events in this book are the products of the author's imagination or are used fictitiously. Any similarity to real persons living or dead is coincidental and not intended by the author.

The views and opinions expressed in this book are solely those of the author and do not reflect the views or opinions of Gatekeeper Press. Gatekeeper Press is not to be held responsible for and expressly disclaims responsibility of the content herein.

The Baker's Legacy: Sequel to The Baker's Daughter

Published by Gatekeeper Press
2167 Stringtown Rd., Suite 109
Columbus, OH 43123-2989
www.GatekeeperPress.com

Copyright © 2022 by Douglas Cornelius
All rights reserved. Neither this book, nor any parts within it may be sold or reproduced in any form or by any electronic or mechanical means, including information storage and retrieval systems, without permission in writing from the author. The only exception is by a reviewer, who may quote short excerpts in a review.

Copyright for the images: iStockphoto.com/Marseas (ruined european city), Ysbrand Cosijn (military officer), Riccardo Cirillo (teen girl)

The editorial work for this book is entirely the product of the author. Gatekeeper Press did not participate in and is not responsible for any aspect of these elements.

Library of Congress Control Number: 2021949483
ISBN (paperback): 9781662921681
eISBN: 9781662921698

Contents

Chapter 1. .1
Chapter 2. 10
Chapter 3. 19
Chapter 4. 24
Chapter 5. 36
Chapter 6. 49
Chapter 7. 59
Chapter 8. 69
Chapter 9. 83
Chapter 10 94
Chapter 11 112
Chapter 12 122
Chapter 13 129
Chapter 14 143
Chapter 15 152
Author Notes 160

Chapter 1

January 1945
Stutthof, Germany

The threat was always there—backbreaking pickax or brickyard duty. What was saving him from one of those? Maybe knowing how to run things. But that skill also led to printing underground leaflets. If they'd been aware of that, little chance he'd be alive today.

Marek Menkowicz pushed the arbor of the drill press down. The new hole in the bracket left a small burr, easily flicked away—like what he'd tried to do to a host of bad memories these last months. Now, thankfully, with few parts left in the bin, he was almost done. These last weeks, things had slowed down at the Focke-Wulff airplane factory in Stutthof. In fact, he had heard talk of the place being shut down. The forced labor of thousands in the plant would come to an end. Then what? To the brickyard?

He shuddered, thinking of working outside in the bitter January cold. But he could survive anything. At age nineteen, he still had his youth going for him. Since he had been recaptured by the Nazis in Berlin and whisked away, with the memory of Liddy's outstretched arms and plaintive call still fresh in his mind, he had persevered. God had given him strength along the way.

That was almost five months ago. Meanwhile, the Russians were no doubt getting closer, if the more frequent explosive battle sounds from the eastern front were any sign.

As anxious thoughts mounted each day, he fought them off by thinking of Liddy. But how was she? Oh, how he wished he could cast aside distressing visions of puffy, tear-filled eyes. He much preferred the resolute jaw jutting forward with determination. Surely, she was somehow guiding the Mittendorf Bakery through these turbulent times. The faith of Klaus and Renate would be a shield holding the family together.

Clang! A box of parts crashed at the station beside him. Brackets tumbled out and skidded across the floor. As if propelled by the forces pulling his thoughts in a hundred directions, they scattered everywhere.

"Dieter," Marek shouted out above the din. "What's happened, old man?" He hurried to help him, wrapping his arm around his drooping shoulders.

"I got careless." A flush crept across Dieter's cheeks as he fell to his knees. His tired arms reached out for parts, but in slow motion.

"I'll help you, no problem." Marek scrambled after the more distant brackets, snatching them up. By the time a guard made his way to the commotion, most of the parts had been retrieved.

"We've got it all under control. Not to worry." Marek offered a smile.

A whistle then blew, and the guards herded factory workers out a single entrance to waiting buses. The bright light stung Marek's eyes, and the blustery wind buffeted his cheeks. Those buses would soon be packed to overflowing and returning to the main camp near Stutthof.

Marek made a point to sit next to Dieter. "Too many months of having to concentrate on the same repetitive task—right, Dieter?"

"You can say that again. I guess my age is finally catching up with me." He ran a hand through his thinning gray hair. "Now I've got this to worry about." He pulled a red slip from his front shirt pocket and flashed it toward Marek. It had a number on it. "Didn't you get one of these?"

"Nope. What's it for?"

"Not sure. But there's rumors that quite a number of us will be marching toward the sea. Can you imagine?"

"No!" Marek's hand came to his chin. "What on earth for?"

"War's winding down. Maybe they want to destroy evidence of all the people in this camp." Dieter shook his head.

"*Achtung*! Listen up," came the stern announcement over a loudspeaker. "At precisely six tomorrow morning, you must be in the courtyard with your red slips. We'll be calling out the numbers of people who will be marching to the coast."

Dieter's suspicion had been confirmed.

The next morning, Marek stood next to Dieter, the cold triggering his wonder whether people without slips needed to be there. He cupped his bare hands and exhaled into them, the moist breath escaping, a small frosty cloud soon disappearing before his eyes. He turned his head to survey the crowd that extended to the far barbed-wire fence. Was it his imagination, or were thousands of eyes gripped with worry staring back at him? He was sure there was nary a smile.

"This will be a long marching trip to the coast, taking seven days," came the disembodied voice over the loudspeaker.

"What happens then?" Dieter whispered to Marek as he fidgeted with his red slip.

"I don't know," Marek replied. "But you'd better not think of the worst, or you'll drive yourself crazy." He rubbed his forehead. "Doesn't mean I'm not worried about you." He bit his lip. "Give it a break, though. That number—you've looked at it so much, you must have memorized it by now."

"I know. Number 3176. If only this were a dream and the number would just disappear like magic."

A new announcement blared, "We will form rows of nine across. Ten rows will be called at a time. Numbers one through ninety, move toward the front gate and make your rows now. *Schnell!*"

"This will take a long time." Marek pitched his voice above the din of all the people in motion. "I wonder what the plans are for the rest of us." He gazed at Dieter, then the man to his right. "Do you have a slip, too?"

Dieter answered for him. "Yes, my good friend Schreiber, here, will be right next to me. He says he'll watch over me."

The man in his fifties offered Marek a curt nod. His dark, bushy mustache, already beginning to frost over, stood out against a pale face whose eyes darted away. He swayed back and forth on his feet. *Was he nervous, or was he just trying to stay warm?*

If only I could warm my feet up as well. But the holes in his boots brought the snow underneath in direct contact with his tattered socks. He tried to flex his toes, but they seemed immovable. *Must think of something warm.*

He imagined pulling loaves of bread out of the warm oven at the Mittendorf Bakery. Liddy would be nearby, her blue eyes admiring the crusty tops, her stubby nose with one grand inhale taking in the glorious aromas wafting through the air. Oh, what he would give to be there. Oh, what he would give to have just one bite. To see Liddy once again.

"This sure makes me reflect about my youth," Dieter interrupted as if trying to be upbeat. "Just like when *I* was a youngster, my granddaughter would probably think this is one grand winter wonderland—but only for about ten minutes." He tried to smile, but it flattened into a grimace.

A gust of wind in front of them swirled up some snowflakes that had not yet been trampled down. Marek turned his head to keep them from stinging his eyes.

"Tell me about your family." His eyes probed his companion.

"Well, I have a son and a daughter, both married, with three grandchildren in total. But we're all separated." A sheen darkened his brown eyes. "I pray they are okay—just don't know their whereabouts."

"Probably the case for most people here," Schreiber added. "I have no children, but do I ever long to see my wife." His eyes gazed off into the distance.

They continued to talk, but the time passed slowly. Shivering while standing in one place made the minutes seem like hours. Many rows now stood in line before them—more than Marek could count. At last, the moment came when Dieter's and Schreiber's numbers were called.

When Schreiber started to move, Marek, without a word, snatched the red slip from the unsuspecting Dieter's hand and hurried to the old man's spot in the line-up. With a reassuring smile, he glanced back.

"What are you doing...?" came Dieter's puzzled cry behind him as he looked in awe of what had just happened.

A symphony of squeaky crunches from thousands of boots compressing the snow on the road filled the crisp air. The rays from the sun, although well above the horizon, provided scant warmth. But what little came their way was most welcome.

"That was a magnanimous gesture you did for Dieter."

Marek shrugged as Schreiber turned to his left from his spot at the far right of their row. "Well, we don't know what's in store for him, but it has to be better than this. He wouldn't have survived this kind of trek." Marek craned toward his new friend. "So, how are you doing?"

"I'm getting by." Schreiber exhaled loudly, his shoulders sinking with his motion. "Not sure I can go on for another six days, though."

Marek studied Schreiber's face. He had given his hat to a young child. Now his ears were a bright red. His bushy gray eyebrows matched his mustache—both frosted over. "I'll be praying for you."

Time was impossible to tell. Only the location of the sun gave him hints. The repetitive strides, one after another, of the man ahead of Marek became mesmerizing. The long day of marching finally ended as, with the setting sun, they were allowed to rest by the wayside among some mature pine trees.

Marek sat with his back against a trunk. But there was no meal to assuage the hunger pangs rumbling in his stomach.

The following day brought a cloudy sky, but it served as a blanket to keep the warmth in. Marek studied Schreiber's stride. On this day, an occasional stumble interrupted its cadence. He put his arm on his friend's shoulder. "Keep at it. You'll be okay," he encouraged as new snowflakes steadily landed, then melted, on their faces.

On the fourth day, they finally received a meal. *Thank God*, Marek thought, even though it was just stale bread and soup with something unidentifiable floating in it. The meal did not bring an added bounce to their steps. No, each one was still a trudging attempt to navigate new ruts in the snow, well-trodden from the marchers before him.

By the fifth day, weariness had set in with most of the marchers, with toes frozen and without feeling. Strides turned into frequent stumbles, especially where the road underneath became uneven. But then the unthinkable happened. Schreiber collapsed to his knees, and before Marek could pull him back up, the SS guard had hit the side of his head with his rifle butt. Schreiber jumped back up, but after a second such incident, he struggled to regain his footing. Marek reached over to help him.

"Keep moving," the guard called out. It seemed those were the only words he knew.

By the afternoon, others began falling by the wayside. Forced to keep moving ahead, Marek was not sure if they got back up again. But he feared the worst. Alas, Schreiber's legs gave out once again. The guard slammed another blow to the head.

"Schreiber, get up! You must keep going," Marek yelled out as he broke rank to help him to his feet. But he, too, received a blow to his head, and his friend slipped out of his grasp. When Schreiber did not get up, the guard kicked him into the ditch at the side of the road. *No, it can't be! Not this. No!* Marek winced long and deep. *Goodbye, my dear friend*, he bemoaned, his head twisted in a longing gaze back. *I did not know you well, but we did indeed have a common bond. God bless you!*

The monotonous marching continued, interrupted only by occasional artillery fire to the east. The Red Army, the Russians, no doubt. Marek was not sure if that was a good thing. But anything had to be better than this. On the tenth day, three days longer than planned, the sight of water, the Baltic Sea, graced their eyes. An overwhelming peace cascaded down Marek's body. *Was it from reaching their destination or seeing God's beautiful creation?* But the peace from the serene waters was short-lived.

Far behind many of the other prisoners as Number 3176, Marek strained to see what was happening. Thousands of marchers before him were herded into the sea. A volley of gunfire from the guards was unleashed. What sort of evil prompted that?

God, please deliver our souls from this bloodbath!

Chapter 2

Warm in the family bakery where they resided, Liddy approached her eleven-year-old brother at the piano bench and massaged his shoulders from behind. He released a deep sigh.

"Willy, you played so beautifully this morning. Too bad Herr Keppler wasn't around to admire it."

"Yeah, I know. I miss him." Willy swiveled on the bench, his lips scrunched up. "He helped me so much with my piano. For a Nazi officer, he always had a sparkle in his eye when I played. Even though he would sit way back there." He cast a crisp nod toward a far table.

"He was so proud of his protégé." Liddy ran a hand through her hair, long strands catching on her callused fingertips. "But it's not just Herr Keppler who's missing—seems like the number of customers is just plain dwindling."

She carried a pile of dishtowels to a table for folding. "It goes back to January," she continued. "Ever since the Russians made that major advance, I feel like all of Berlin is just going through the motions, waiting for the inevitable downfall."

"Then what happens when we lose the war?"

"We're just ordinary citizens, Willy—not Nazis, like Herr Keppler. That's how they'd better look at us. We just have to keep praying that things will work out. I pray for Father's safety every day."

Mother Renate came out of the kitchen and cast a disparaging look their way.

"No time for chitchat this morning," she said. "Those tables over there need a good cleaning." She rubbed the back of her neck. "And, Willy, go find your broom. You're the man of the house now. Make your father proud of you." When she assigned duties, it wasn't just with the Mittendorf family bakery in mind. This was also their home.

He clomped from his seat to the closet. "When do you suppose we'll hear from Father?" The strain in his voice matched the pinch to his forehead as he pulled a broom from the closet and began sweeping.

"Hard to say," Mother replied. "I trust he's okay." She turned away and mumbled, "I just wish the Führer hadn't come up with that *Volksturm* idea—pushing regular people, old and young, out to the frontline."

Liddy picked up on her muffled comment as she repositioned some pastries in the display case. "Just shows how bad times have become."

Willy leaned on the broom, tucking the handle to his quivering chin, eyes wider. "I thought Father's prison-guard job was supposed to keep him safe?"

"Not any longer." Mother grimaced as she wiped a table with gusto.

"I miss the tidbits of moral instruction he relayed from Herr Bonhoeffer," Liddy added. "Sometimes they brightened my day."

"If only we had another capable body around here," Mother mused. "Someone like Marek."

Liddy's hand flinched, tipping a coffee cup over on a tray of dirty dishes.

"Oh, so sorry, Liddy. I didn't mean to…"

"That's all right." Liddy closed her eyes, taking a deep breath as flashes of Marek popped into her head. The image of his kneading bread with flair was soon replaced by one of him charging ahead of her on his bike. She forced a sad smile at her mother. "I adored him. The bad part is how it all ended up." Her bottom lip trembled. "Getting whisked away at the very moment we were to be re-reunited. A person can never forget that. Never!"

"Do you think Marek is still okay?" Willy toyed with the broom, doing little more than kicking up dust as he frowned at the wooden floor.

"I pray to God he is, but I don't know God's plan for him." She looked upward at a crack in the plaster ceiling new from last week's bombings. "This war has been such a dreadful experience...." She paused. "The sad part is, even though it's coming to an end, I'm afraid the dread will continue for some time."

～

All week long, Liddy had heard the ever-increasing artillery fire reverberate just outside of town. As she lay in bed half-asleep in the early-morning hours, a new sound awoke her. A whirring mechanical noise penetrated her room, and she sat straight up, startled.

"Oh, no, no, no," she blurted. "They're here! Mother, no." She bolted from bed. "They're here! Mother, Willie! Get up!" She rushed to her bedroom window. A tank crawled down the street. Grabbing her stomach, she gasped for air. *Oh, dear God, help us!*

"The Russians are here. The Russians are here," she kept shouting.

Her mother, who had been sleeping on the sofa in the side room downstairs, yelled up to her, "I'll double check the front door lock." A ragged catch stopped her voice from carrying as well as it usually did. "Make sure Willy gets up.... No... maybe he should stay in his room. Keep most of the lights off. Let's make it look like no one is home."

Liddy joined her on a chair next to the sofa. She just stared at her. How could it be? This day was finally here. Why couldn't it be just another air raid? They had that drill down pat. They sat in silence in their bathrobes, but the noise outside got louder. Soldiers yelling to one another carried through the door.

A sharp blow of something to the front door shook the entire entryway. Another one, then another, followed by boot kicks. The lock finally gave way, and the door burst open. A scream jumped from Liddy's throat. She sprang to her feet, knocking the chair back a few inches as she hurried to put an arm around her mother.

Three soldiers entered. The flurry of Russian words rattling off their lips left no doubt this was more than an invasion of their privacy—it was a foreign invasion. Light from a flashlight bounced around the walls, highlighting a silver streak in one of the soldier's hair. They spotted the pastry case, and a rifle butt soon smashed it open, pieces of shattered glass flying across the floor. Liddy jumped up toward the case.

"Yes, yes, there's plenty of food here." She gestured with her hand coming to her mouth. "Take what you want." *Just don't hurt us.* But she dared not say it. Then she spotted Willy peering down from the top of the stairs. "Get back in your bedroom, Willy," she ordered. "And lock the door."

The soldiers scarfed down some day-old pastries, their smiles suggesting they were satisfied. But they were not done. The leader stalked her, blood oozing out from a cut on the top of his hand.

"No, no," she whispered, backing up a step.

"Stop! Don't you dare touch my daughter," her mother shrieked, lunging to her feet and rushing forward. "Stop." She flung her arm out, but it was soon captured by the strong grasp of the soldier's hand. Her mother struggled in vain against the man who restrained her.

"Please… No!" Liddy backed into a table and scrambled around it, placing a paltry café chair between them. A mere swipe from the stalker sent the chair flying. The brute of a soldier snatched her watch off her wrist and clutched at her bathrobe belt. Her mother shrieked again.

Liddy fainted.

An eerie quiet returned to the household. All except for Liddy's plaintive sobbing, which continued for hours. She had been assaulted, violated, and ravaged—the worst thing imaginable. She lay on the sofa, her head propped up by a small pillow, already damp. The windows rattled from the strong wind outside.

Is that all, God? Rattling some windows? Can't You be more upset? Why are You so far away? Oh, I wish Father were here. Where is he? I need his embrace! Her mother kept trying to comfort her. "I feel so defiled and unworthy, Mother." Her mother stroked her back as she tried to engage her in prayer, but Liddy's thoughts were in total disarray.

"Pray, liebchen, pray." Her mother's soft voice kept repeating.

Pray? Liddy couldn't focus. *Who was this God who allowed this to happen?*

Willy scuffled down the stairs. "Are you all right, Liddy? What happened? I stayed in my room with the door locked until the noise stopped."

Liddy tried to respond, but the words were lost in her continued crying.

"The soldiers…" Her mother's voice clogged. She coughed and whimpered before trying again. "Those soldiers… they… treated your sister horribly."

"What happened? What about you, Mother? Are you okay?"

"Don't worry about me." She released a loud sigh. "But your poor sister here is devastated." She reached for him and gave him a hug. "I tried to help, but… we won't talk about it now. Maybe some other time. Appears the Russians have taken over Berlin. But don't worry." She tried to sound positive, covering up a fist clenched by her other hand. "Why don't you go back upstairs to your room and try to get some sleep?"

Willy gazed at the smashed pastry case, shook his head, and trudged up the stairs. He looked back and asked, "What does that mean about Father?"

"We just don't know, son."

"And Herr Keppler. I worry about him, too."

Through the morning hours, they lay together on the sofa. Her mother's warm embrace had sustained her. Liddy rubbed her scratchy eyes. They were dry now. All the tears had been shed. *Oh, how her body ached*! Yes, the Russian intruders were long gone, but what was next? As her mother stirred, she hugged her, then, ignoring the dull pains of her body, headed to the window without a word. *Had this all been a bad dream?* Pushing the curtain aside, she looked out at two soldiers standing across the street. *No, this hadn't been a dream.* But now a quiet persisted, in marked contrast to the noise just hours before. As for the two soldiers, they were not the ones who had been there when she was ravaged.

Her mother walked over, brushed Liddy's hair aside, and probed into her eyes. At length, she lowered her head, her already slouched shoulders curving inward yet farther, the sheen in her eyes leaking down her cheeks. She finally spoke.

"I don't know what to say, my sweet Liddy. I wish I could have helped more, protected you...." She fisted her hands as her voice quivered. "This war has been one long nightmare. Just when you think it can't get any worse, it does. Why has God let this happen? I keep asking, but I just don't know. I guess we should thank Him for surviving to this point." A long exhale followed.

"It's so hard to do when these kinds of things happen." Liddy stared at the floor as she pulled the belt to her bathrobe tight, really tight.

Chapter 3

For three months, Marek suffered nightmares about the execution of thousands in the Baltic Sea. Why had they stopped shooting and herded the survivors back to Stutthof? Now, hearing another trip to the sea was planned, he couldn't stop shaking. But then rumors circulated about an evacuation. Were the Nazis trying to hide the evidence of hundreds of thousands of abused prisoners?

Loaded onto barges, elbows jabbing each other, the prisoners were now headed toward another ship in Neustadt Bay.

"I wonder what kind of ship they're going to herd us onto?" a companion next to him asked. "I'll bet it's some sort of fishing trawler that reeks to high heaven."

As they passed a tugboat, from a distance Marek sighted three large smokestacks of what appeared to be an ocean liner. "Maybe we'll be fortunate enough to get on that one." He nodded toward it, taking in a deep breath.

"No way. After everything we've been through? We should be so lucky!"

As they approached closer, Marek's hopes were confirmed. *Had some general been overwhelmed with guilt? Were the Germans going to be decent about how they evacuated them? Or was my imagination getting carried away?* The ship's bold lettering now stood out—*Cap Arcona*.

As Marek boarded with his acquaintance, he gripped the wooden railing. Its satin-smooth finish glided beneath his palm—high quality. This was no dream. The ship was indeed intended for trans-ocean travel.

A guard pointed for them to all head down the long deck. "Go all the way to the farthest available room."

Marek swung his arms as he almost skipped, jostling past his companion. Yes, everything considered, it was a good day. But then guilt set in. He wondered about Liddy and her family. More frequent bombings, no doubt, meant more trips to the cellar, each one increasingly difficult for her arthritic mother. Were they strong enough to get through it all?

∽

Later that afternoon, on *Cap Arcona*'s main deck with his friend, Marek just shook his head as hordes of prisoners kept boarding. "I'm afraid actual living conditions will be in sharp contrast to the vessel's upscale trappings."

"No doubt with severe overcrowding." His companion, Brandt, gripped the rail and leaned far over the side.

Along with thousands of passengers, hundreds of SS guards, as well as a naval gunnery detail, climbed the gangway. The prospect of a decent meal seemed to fade with each new boarder—not to mention a shortage of fresh water. When water was finally doled out, Brandt insisted that Marek, looking dehydrated, take some of his.

Days later, the waves of new passengers finally ceased. "I wonder if the ship is at any risk of sinking due to overloading?" He rubbed his jaw. "I've made a point of locating the stations where the life vests are stored. We should make sure others do, too."

Brandt nodded in agreement.

The next day, as they all waited for the ship to disembark, Marek surveyed the faces of his friend and other people around them. Many were forlorn. Others were just blank, apparently resigned to the next step in this miserable journey. Marek couldn't tell if cheeks were sullen and sunken due to hunger or perhaps to illness. Back at Stutthof, typhus had once decimated the ranks. How quickly it would spread if it started in these tight quarters.

On the afternoon of May 3, the distant drone of approaching aircraft came as a surprise.

"What do you suppose that's from?" Brandt asked. The look of concern on the ruddy face of his companion in his mid-fifties was startling. "The Luftwaffe has not been very active in recent months."

More unbelievable than the pending evacuation and escape on an ocean liner would be an attack by Allied planes. Marek grabbed his friend's arm and met his eyes with an incredulous stare. The British RAF strafed the ship with artillery fire, bombs, and even rockets. Another wave followed. Marek craned closer to the railing, lifting on his toes—could they not see the white flags hoisted high above the deck?

"They must think these are enemy troops trying to escape. Duck, Marek!"

In a flash after his friend's shout, Marek thudded to the deck. A deafening nearby explosion reverberated in his ears, and the weight of Brandt landed on top of him. Marek waited for him to gather himself.

"Brandt? Are you all right?"

No answer.

"Brandt, buddy. Let me help you get back up." As Marek rolled his body to a sitting position, his worst fears were realized.

Brandt lay motionless, with no sign of a pulse.

Marek grimaced and bowed his head, trying to mumble a short prayer. Had a man he barely knew saved his life? Why had Marek been faster to get down? Did his youthful quickness mean Brandt had paid the price?

Soon many parts of the *Cap Arcona* were ablaze. A heaviness in his chest, Marek said a quiet goodbye to his friend and then rushed to the life-vest station. He handed out as many as he could. Small rescue boats were lowered into the cold waters. Many terror-stricken inmates did not wait for the boats and jumped right in.

After another wave of attacks, Marek donned a life vest. Not daring to wait any longer, he dove in.

Man, this water is cold. His senses took a moment to absorb the shock.

People thrashed beside him. "Help," came a cry from an older lady.

He tried to assist her as she struggled to board a lifeboat. But even those boats were the targets of gunfire from a new wave of aircraft above.

I've got to get away from the burning target of the ship. He swam toward shore as fast as he could.

Reaching the shoreline, he hoisted his cold and weary body out of the water. Behind him, the massive ship had sunk in the shallow water, but its upper structure was still ablaze. Frantic rowers guided their rescue boats toward shore. More bodies were floating face down than he could count. *Oh, the humanity*! His body shook.

He had heard about the sinking of the *Titanic* years before and imagined this is what it must have looked like. *And now the* Cap Arcona. His heart raced. He shivered as he dropped down to his knees. *Thank You, God, for delivering me from this inferno, and bless those who have been lost, especially Brandt.*

Chapter 4

Liddy, Renate, and Willy gathered around the radio in the side room to hear the formal announcement. Liddy would never forget the date—May 7.

"...the Supreme Command of the Wehrmacht today has declared the unconditional capitulation of all fighting troops...."

"So it's official." She straightened, lifting her chin. "Maybe this means we'll see Father walk through that door soon. I–I need him to tell me once again that everything is going to be okay. That God is in charge."

The afternoon of the second day following Germany's surrender, two Russian soldiers appeared at the front door. The scowl on Renate's face matched the one she had shown to Nazi officer Keppler when he first showed up at the family bakery a few years before. Liddy stood by a table in the background. The hands in her apron pockets shook so badly, she thrust them even deeper. She couldn't look at the two soldiers.

"What do you want?" Renate asked.

"Bread," one of them replied in broken German, his wide lips turning flat, his dark eyes focused. "You must make bread for the people." He gestured toward others out in the street. He pulled a card from his back pocket and handed it to her.

"Why, this is a ration card." She lowered and then passed it to Liddy. As Liddy stepped forward, the other soldier removed his cap to wipe his brow with the top of his hand. The sun glistened against the damp pink of a healing scar. Their eyes met.

"Ohhh." Her hand slapped forward to cover her eyes. Weakened, she stumbled back to sit, her head shaking, her stomach quaking.

"You'll feed people," the first soldier continued. "We'll get you supplies and instructions."

⸻

Marek couldn't take the backroads. Too many people were on the move—prisoners on a forced march, SS guards, even the Russians. No doubt, his Polish home was east, though, so he'd head toward the rising sun even at the risk of running into Russians. After all, weren't they supposed to be liberators? They'd have more sympathy for him than desperate SS guards who would fire their rifles first and ask questions later.

So he'd stay out of sight, traveling from tree to tree through the woods alongside the roads, careful not to linger in any bright shafts of sunlight. Fortunately, since it was May, chattering teeth and numb fingers and toes were things of the past.

Now his stomach was well beyond the point of growling—it was twisting in famished knots. In a clearing beyond the woods, the gabled peak of a farmhouse rose above the field. *Dare I approach it?* If the family were Nazi sympathizers, bitter about how the war was ending, disaster might be imminent. He moved closer to inspect any signs. No flags, no swastikas, no harbingers of anything having to do with the Third Reich.

He continued walking, saying a short prayer as he approached. At last, with a loud exhale, he knocked on the door. At first, there was no answer. He knocked again.

An older woman's voice warbled from the other side. "Who's there?"

"My name's Marek. I need help." He grimaced when he didn't hear an immediate response.

"What's happened?" the query finally came, barely audible.

"I'm a refugee. I'm starving." The words had trouble escaping from his dry mouth.

"You're not a Russian, are you?"

"No, no." Good thing his German was perfect, his Polish accent long since surrendered. "Please, I beg you to let me in." He anxiously wiped his feet on the mat.

The door opened. A lady of medium build and graying hair stood before him wearing a soiled apron.

"Oh my, aren't you a sight? Come in, and I'll see what I can find." She closed the door behind him. "My husband is due back any minute now."

"Bless you for letting me in." His eyes tipped heavenward as he grabbed the doorframe to steady himself.

The lady's head perked up. "I have some stew in the oven. Let me see.... I'll need to set out another place setting. Help yourself to some water. Take this glass, and there's a pitcher in the refrigerator."

He emptied the pitcher, but when he went to refill it, he paused at how badly the faucet was leaking. "Oops. Looks like this needs a new washer or seal."

"Yes, it's getting pretty bad. Go ahead and sit down while I serve up some stew."

Marek collapsed into a chair. Relieved to be off his feet, he exhaled loudly as he surveyed the older appliances and badly worn countertop. He fit right in.

With only two place settings at the table, he saw no sign yet of her husband. Then a side door creaked open, and a young lady stepped into the kitchen.

"This is my daughter, Freda. She doesn't make an appearance until she feels comfortable." Freda offered a demure smile, then retrieved silverware from a drawer.

"Well, I'm glad you don't perceive me as a threat." There was no response—only extended quiet. *I must engage this dear woman in conversation.* "Um, what do you grow around here?"

"Mostly potatoes—we have a variety of them. Plus, a few other things. It's still early, though." She paused, ladle in hand as she glanced his way. "So, what's your background?"

"I was born a Polish Jew," he mumbled as she pulled the stew from the oven. The aroma overwhelmed his senses—it had been so long. Maybe he shouldn't have answered. Not before she let him eat.

"Polish, huh? So am I. My husband's German. We're not that far from Poland now, you know." She set the pot on the stovetop with a nod, her demeanor seeming more comfortable with him.

"Praise God—that's where I'm headed. I escaped from a forced labor camp near Stutthof."

The lady shook her head and wrinkled her nose. "That Hitler sure did some horrible things to you folks. I've seen the train cars of people—loaded up like cattle."

"You haven't seen the worst of it." His voice cracked.

"So, what did you say your name was?" Her eyes now seemed wider and shining.

"Marek... And you are?"

"Frau Stolle." She brought three plates laden with stew to the table.

"I'd be happy to pray," he offered.

After the prayer, she remarked, "You sure sound like a believer in Jesus Christ."

"I am." He made direct eye contact with her as he nodded.

"Wonderful. I've been praying a lot the last few years."

"I think a great many of us have." He let out a heavy exhale. He drew in his first bite. His initial chews were slow and deliberate. They unleashed flavors he had not enjoyed for many a month. Bits of fresh ground pepper tingled the tip of his tongue. But then the pull of his growling stomach overwhelmed his desire to linger and savor the exquisite flavors. One bite followed right after another, in increasingly rapid succession. Except for the sound of silverware scraping their plates, silence dominated the next minutes.

"I can't tell you how much this means to me." Marek finally lowered his fork and reached for the water glass. "I was famished."

"Well, I wish I had more. I didn't make very much." Her voice faded.

"Frau Stolle, may I ask you a question?" He didn't wait for an answer. "Do you really expect Herr Stolle home tonight?"

Her face turned red, and soon tears burst down her cheeks before she buried her face in her hands. "No, no, he was a war casualty. I didn't know if I could trust you."

"Oh, that's all right. I'm the one who is sorry—so sorry for your loss." Freda arose from her chair and wrapped a comforting arm around her mother. While Frau Stolle whimpered, he searched for something to break the tension. "Say, when we're done eating, I'd like to try to fix that." He pointed toward the dripping faucet. "It's the least I could do. I presume your husband had some tools, washers and the like?"

"Yes, in the barn. That would be so nice of you."

"So how do you manage to keep this farm going?"

"I know someone who has some teenage boys. They come over and help."

"Terrific." He subconsciously offered a thumbs-up and agreed when she later asked if he would like to stay overnight. The following morning, she prepared breakfast and invited him to stay several more days. "You know, those teenaged boys I spoke about are not the most reliable," she asserted.

Later that afternoon, while Marek was in the barn, the door opened, and Freda entered. Wearing crisp blue dungarees, she closed the door behind her and approached.

"What are you working on?" she asked, her eyelashes fluttering, and bright blue eyes bringing a fresh sparkle to the languid hours of the afternoon.

"Oh, with that faucet done, I thought I'd work on sharpening the business end of this potato picker."

"Well, I just wanted you to know how much my mother and I appreciate your being around. I can't tell you how much it means to her." She gazed down, hesitated, then raised her head back up.

"And to me. Will you consider staying on—at least for a short while?"

"We'll see. I certainly don't want to leave you and your mother in a lurch."

After three days, the temptation to stay longer was superseded by an irresistible pull to get back. He resumed his journey, but only after getting a special blessing from Frau Stolle—so special that it echoed in his mind for hours.

In the bakery, Liddy moved from one task to another, unable to focus. She frowned at a stack of papers on the kitchen table. Depositing the last one from her hand to the top of the pile, she gave it a final gentle tap.

"Willy, will you file all these recipes in the drawer? We won't be needing them." She shook her head with a sigh.

"You mean we're not going to be making any more marble ryes with the signature *M* on the top? Marek would be sad to hear that."

Her energy dipped a notch lower. "No, I'm afraid not," her flat voice came back. "I can only pray Marek is around to be sad someday when he hears about that."

"Yes, I'll say. And Herr Keppler, too. What do you suppose has happened to him?"

"Well, I imagine he's been captured by the Russians and is on his way to a prisoner-of-war camp. He was a Nazi officer. They might charge him with crimes against humanity."

"Herr Keppler? He told me once he'd never killed anyone. And then he let Marek out of jail. He ended up on our side."

"Thank God for that!" She began to wipe the table clean, then stopped and faced Willy, seated at the table. "Hey, I have an idea. Maybe you could write to somebody and put in a good word for him."

Willy's head jerked up, his eyes widened, and a smile erupted on his face. "Really? They'd read a letter from someone like me?" He stood up and paced around the table. "Well, then, I'll have to use my best penmanship Where would I send it to?"

"I don't know. I'll see if I can find out." A warmth radiated through her body as she pondered the possibility. "Anyway, getting back to the recipes, there's only one thing we're going to be making—a plain white loaf of bread. We have to make as many as we can to sustain a lot of hungry people. Folks will be given a ration card to present to us. Schools will remain closed for some time, so you and Mother need to help me in the morning."

The heavyset man with thinning hair had sought him out, even though the man was certainly much younger. Keppler did not know why, what with the thousands of detainees in the prisoner-of-war camp to choose from.

Maybe in some brief conversation, the man had decided Keppler, too, was well educated. Certainly, his appeal was not a shared joy over the fall of the Third Reich. Even with the war over, the man, Fredrik Bernhard, came across as a devout Nazi soldier.

He bragged about being educated at the university in civil engineering. His family came from Dresden, as did Keppler's.

"So, what did you say you taught at the university?" Bernhard asked, settling in beside him on a large fallen tree trunk.

"Music, both history and theory." Keppler raised his eyebrows in search of a reaction.

"Oh, then I'm pretty sure I didn't take any of your courses." Bernhard half laughed as he turned away trying to hide a smirk.

A smirk of his own curled Keppler's lips. "I won't hold it against you. Any man from Dresden is still a man of splendid heritage."

"How long do you suppose we're banished to this dump?" Bernhard stuck his nose up as if to get a reminder of the horrid odor.

"Who knows? I imagine they're having a tough time trying to sort out who is who."

"Well, I think they've figured out who I am. They know they're going to need me to rebuild this country."

That would be a comfortable feeling. "I don't imagine they have any use for me." Keppler brushed the dust off his boots. "I'm just a fastidious, former music professor pushed into being a Nazi officer because I loved my country. I happened to be hung up on precision, discipline, and routine. I just hope they don't decide I'm a war criminal. I could tell when the final stanza was about to be played."

"Really?" Bernhard paused. "You gave up on the Führer?"

"Yep, there's some things more important than *his* kind of country." Keppler frowned as his lips pressed tight. "I was appalled by what the Jews endured."

"I can't say we've got it much better here." Bernhard crossed his arms.

You won't be heavyset for long.

The rain was relentless. As if God wanted to wash away any remnant of the horror perpetrated upon the Polish people. *Rain on*, thought Marek, *rain on*. He stopped to press the toe of his boot from side to side in the mud, grinding it the way he would snuff out a bug. He had lost track of how many days he had trudged on, one stride after another, since getting a meal at Frau Stolle's home. He tried knocking on other farmhouse doors, but none ever opened. Some familiar landmarks, however, promised Warsaw couldn't be much farther. Of course, whether the building where he had lived would be intact, he knew not.

He prayed his parents would be headed there as well—hopefully, they'd already beat him.

He had tried to catch a ride on a freight car, but the few that trundled along were overloaded with foodstuffs trying to make it to hungry markets.

How ironic. If only one of those trains would stop to feed a starving man on foot. He wasn't getting the nourishment his weary body craved. He found his stride getting shorter, his knees weaker, and his curved back dragging his head closer to the ground.

Finally, his head found the ground.

With daylight breaking the next morning, three soldiers peered over him, brandishing weapons and peppering him with questions. They were not speaking German—no doubt, it must be Russian.

"Don't shoot, don't shoot," was his first reaction with a hollow cracking voice, but they appeared not to understand. He tried to raise his arms in surrender but was too weak to do so.

Chapter 5

Marek felt the tug of strong hands under each armpit, and the backside of his body scraping along the rough terrain. Where were they dragging him to? Some cliff to be thrown over?

His back was soon propped up against something hard, his head now bobbing against what must have been the bark of a large tree. Slaps each side of his cheeks became more intense, finally arousing him from his stupor.

What made him realize he must abandon trying to respond in German, he knew not. "Don't hurt me. I need help," he kept repeating in Polish. Their animated Russian voices followed, getting louder as they appeared to argue amongst themselves.

In the end, he never knew why the soldiers left him unharmed. Why they gave him water and fed him. They must have figured he was a harmless war victim, not a Nazi soldier. Had they not come along when they did, he believed there was no way he would have survived.

On this late-May morning, the line stretched out farther than usual. Liddy filled a basket full of bread loaves and headed outside to hand them out in exchange for a check-off on a ration card. But then she cringed, the basket falling to the ground. There he was, back again, admiring the line of people. Ivan was his name. She couldn't look at him. Fear and loathing took over her senses as the hair on the nape of her neck lifted. She ground her teeth. He approached her saying "hello," and when she refused to look up, he grasped her chin, brusquely forcing her to acknowledge him.

"I need to talk to you," he said in broken German, his shoulders broad and stiff.

"Little chance of that," she shrilled, trying to lean away.

"Yes, we must talk." He squeezed her arm, and then pulled her several paces away from the line of people.

"You seem to have your breadline working well." He gazed back at the folks anxiously awaiting their turn.

What is he up to with this hollow compliment?

"Is that all you came here to tell me?" For a moment, she stared at him intensely, her jaw clenched, then turned her head away.

"No, hear me out. I came to tell you something about that night." His jaw jutted out below determined eyes.

"What?" Her chest tightened, and goose bumps shivered down her arms.

"I'm sorry for what I did." He reached to grasp her hand, but she shielded it from his touch behind her back.

"Okay, you've said it." She wrinkled her nose. "You expect me to believe you? Now please leave me alone."

"No. I was truly hoping to keep seeing you." He lowered his chin and kicked a pebble across the street. "But on better terms."

What! Bile rose up her throat, her knees started shaking, and her hands fisted. "You've got to be crazy." Her jaw clenched. "How can I possibly be friends with you? After everything that you did?" As if that didn't make enough sense, she slid the treasured photo of Marek from her pocket and flashed it toward him. Pride flared through her. "*I* already have someone."

"I don't see him around. I'm here. I want to be the one. Please?"

For the first time, is he sounding sincere?

Liddy stammered and shook her head as tears welled up in her eyes. The harder she shook, the firmer his grasp of her wrists, his fingernails now digging in.

"No way!" she blurted out. "You've hurt me. Now stay away, or I'll report you. I know where your bosses are." She pointed a finger like a knife. "I'm not afraid to go to them."

But, surely, her outburst meant she was on a stage and onlookers were taking it all in. She glanced down the line to see if she'd spot some familiar faces. The wide eyes of a neighbor boy who used to play with Willy were fixated on her. But at this time, she was in no mood to explain or exchange pleasantries.

She ran back into the bakery.

⌒

Sunlight warmed his face, easing away the bleakness that had claimed a spot in his soul. June, somehow no different from the many before it and the many to come after it, promised the hope of summer as fields spread alongside the country road. After tipping his head to it, Keppler drew a deep breath and eyed Bernhard as the truck jostled, and someone's elbow struck his midsection. No apology came from the burly man beside him. How out of place he felt compared to the men sharing the back of the truck with him. "Why did you pick me, Bernard?"

"I wanted someone else with a head on his shoulders." Bernhard fiddled with the handle of a hammer he held. "These other guys—I picked them for their muscles." He smiled at the three burly men across from him who seemed unamused by the comment.

Keppler shifted, trying to keep his tailbone from cracking as the truck struck a pothole. "But I know nothing about repairing railway tracks."

"You'll be a fast learner." Bernhard tossed the hammer into a toolbox at his feet and slammed the lid shut with authority.

As they approached the site and came to a stop, the guard in the front passenger seat jumped out first. The Russian man could not speak any German but mumbled something and motioned with his arms as if to say "get to work."

They unloaded several lengths of rail and multiple cross ties. Bernhard examined the segment of track and determined which pieces to replace.

"Look here." He motioned to Keppler. "Even though the bombs didn't directly hit the tracks, they were close enough to disturb the underlying ground. Without the right support, and with some heavy rains, the rails have given way a bit."

Keppler joined the others with his shovel, glad to know they could carry the bulk of the heavy workload.

Another day, another breadline. Pleased to spot some familiar faces, she let a long-absent smile return to her face. They were the people she wanted to see—not Russians. Today, it was moving faster than usual. Maybe because Willy was helping her hand out the loaves.

"I think we've got this routine figured out." She shielded her eyes from the bright morning sun, then nudged his shoulder. "But I bet you'd rather be in school. Who knows when they'll start that up again?"

"No, I feel good about this—because we're helping people." A deep, gratifying sigh followed.

"Yes." She wiped her forehead with the back of her hand. "I only hope we can keep the supply of flour and other ingredients coming from the authorities. The need is so great."

Frau Bauer, a short lady from the neighborhood, stepped forward to greet her. "Oh, Liddy," she said with a soft voice and pleading eyes. "I don't have my ration card with me, but my family is famished."

Liddy raised her head above the crowd and scanned for any Russian authorities. "Here, Frau Bauer, take this loaf, but next time, bring your card." She tilted her head. "In fact, take two, what's one more?" She shrugged half-heartedly. Next in line came Herr Wolff, whom she hadn't seen in church for quite some time.

"Herr Wolff, so good to see you. I see you're back from your duty with the Volksturm."

He moved closer to whisper. "Yes, don't tell anyone, but I left early. I could see what was going to happen." He shrugged while trying to cover a sheepish look.

A little thrill zinged through her, and she grinned at Willy. "Maybe that means Father will show up soon."

Herr Wolff jerked his head back. "You haven't..." He stopped, pursed his lips, and gazed down. "I... I need to talk to you and your mother. Is she inside?"

Liddy flinched. "What's happened? Do you know where my father is?" She leaned back. When she continued to probe, Herr Wolff remained silent. "Yes, let's go find Mother."

Renate was sitting in the front room at a table, a cup of coffee in her hand.

"Herr Wolff, what brings you to the Mittendorf Bakery? Excuse me if I don't get up and give you the hug I'm sure you deserve."

"Good to see you, Renate. Well, for one thing—I needed this loaf of bread. But there's something more important I have to talk to you about." He nodded at Liddy, and they sat at the table together.

"What is it?" Renate clutched her arm to her chest. "It's about Klaus, isn't it?" The pitch of her voice rose with each word, and Liddy felt her pulse picking up as well. "What's happened to him?"

"Klaus and I were in the same regiment as part of the Volksturm. You know the Russians made that big push back in January. I was right alongside Klaus."

"He's been hurt, hasn't he? Where is he?" Renate fidgeted with a button on her blouse.

"I figured the authorities would have notified you by now." He avoided any eye contact, focusing instead on the wall clock as if he wanted this moment to be past.

Pulse increasing, Liddy tried to connect with him.

"Well, er… I struggle to even say the words…"

Tell us, dear man!

"I'm so sorry to say… Klaus… died in that big January offensive."

Renate shrieked as her coffee cup came smashing down to the table. "Oh, dear God, please no!"

A shrill wail leaped from Liddy's mouth. She closed her eyes and shook her head, the tears streaming down her face. But she couldn't just sit there, not now. She rose and put an arm around her mother, their heads pressed tight together. She couldn't hold her tight enough, lingering, clutching one of the few loved ones she had left.

"Oh, dear Mother," she whispered. "We've lost him—how can it be? No, no, no! Why has God taken him?" She stroked her mother's hair and continued, trying to soothe the pain away.

"I'm so sorry to be the bearer of such horrible news," Wolff lamented. "I sure would have thought you'd know by now. I guess everything is broken." He rubbed his moist forehead. "Not the least of which are some tender hearts. I am so sorry."

Liddy and her mother remained in each other's arms.

⸻

Marek marshaled all his strength in lifting one leg after the other up the apartment stairs. He thought back to the time a few years earlier when he had bounded with great energy up these very stairs only to find the third-floor apartment empty—both his parents mysteriously gone.

Maybe somebody else lives here now. He rapped on the door, its faded wood sounding hollow. No answer. Then another knock.

A weak voice finally vibrated through the door. "Who's there?"

That voice sounded like Mother's!

"Marek," he replied as he stroked the stubble on his chin. The door burst open. Eyes bulged as the thin face, framed by swept-back gray hair, brightened.

"Oh, Marek!" She fell to her knees weeping. He cupped her cheeks, wet and warm, as her eyes gazed upward, canvassing every square inch of his face. "My prayers have been answered! I was afraid this day would never come."

He pulled his mother to her feet and delivered a big hug, his joy abounding with the love that had been stored up through all the years of war. They remained clenched tight, one to the other, for several minutes.

"How sweet this is! Praise God, you've survived," he whispered, almost afraid to say the words too loudly and find them a dream. The two continued to embrace. At last, he dared voice the question he'd been afraid to ask. "And Father?"

His mother shook her head. "I'm still praying, but no sign of him yet, my son." The two words, *my son*, echoed in his mind. Oh, how he loved the sound of those words.

He would have to settle for that until his father could come home to repeat those same words to him, as well.

He scoped out their abode, hoping it had not changed. The olive-green sofa with familiar beige pillows occupied most of one wall in the living room. A stack of papers and mail now covered the wooden dining table. The cutting board on the kitchen counter and the white dishtowel with red roosters reassured him that life was moving on the way he had remembered it.

Later that afternoon, after some bread and juice for nourishment, they sat together on the living-room sofa. He prompted her to share some reflections of being held captive by the Nazis.

"Oh dear," came her response. "It's so difficult, Marek." Her unfocused gaze became glassy and was soon eclipsed by closed eyelids.

"Okay, not the really horrible stuff."

"They showed up out of nowhere on that day back in '42. Just like that, we were gone. Right away, we got separated. I was sent to Auschwitz, then later to Ravensbruck. My faith sustained me—that and the thought of our reunion." Her voice remained soft. "Without a doubt, I was determined to stay strong throughout. Finally, in April, we were liberated, and I made it back here." She slumped on the sofa.

Marek shared about fleeing early to his uncle's in Berlin, his time at the bakery, and his recapture and stint at Stutthof. Afterward, he released a long sigh and eyed her attentive face. "So, Mother, throughout it all, what was your greatest fear?"

She smoothed the front of her pale-yellow housedress. "All the worry about not knowing what was happening to you and your father." Her eyes turned distant and moist as she reached for a handkerchief from her pocket.

"Of course, you know, I worried about the two of you day and night, as well." Marek rested his hand on her arm. "I am so fortunate to have your love. From parents, it's a blessing not all can share." After a moment, he leaned back on the sofa. "But beyond that, Mother, what?"

"Well, seeing all those poor defenseless children being dragged into a pit of evil on no account of their own was horrific. They depended on adults in this world who failed them. What should have been lives filled with love were snuffed out." Her painful stare persisted.

His shoulders sloped, a terrible weight accompanying her words. "Children depend on unending love from start to finish." As she continued, Marek's mind flashed back to his childhood when Mother had hugged him after he scraped his knee. That thought prompted him to jump from the sofa.

"Hey, I've got to see my old bedroom."

He had not been in that room for a couple of years. His mother followed him like a puppy, as if not wanting to let anything separate her from her newfound son. When they were together in the room, he looked around, refreshing his memory of the sturdy bed with a navy-blue bedspread, the comfortable old chair, and the reading lamp.

With his hand, he brushed dust flecks off the dresser top and pulled the upper drawer open. His eyes widened at the sight of one of his treasures—his prized coin collection. It was still there! He picked up a coin, examining it, but his smile turned serious. The luster was no longer there—the metal tarnished. He tried to wipe it clean. Like the memories of the last few years of his life, the tarnish could not be easily removed.

He turned to his mother and sighed deeply. A coin in hand, he took a seat in his favorite brown chair while she plopped on his bed, her feet on top as well.

He searched for her eyes. "So, Mother, can I ask you another question? After everything we've been through, do you think maybe we've changed?" He paused as his eyes moistened. "Do you think—how should I put it?—that we're da–maged goods?" He continued to rub the coin hard with his thumb. "I guess what I'm trying to ask is, am I still the *same old Marek*?" He shifted in his chair, the soft corduroy crinkling with his movement.

She sat up, put her feet on the floor, and cocked her head to the side. Her shoulders curled forward. "Well, after what we've been through, we can't help but be different." She took a half-hearted swipe at the dusty headboard—that she'd missed it in her earlier cleaning proved how much she'd changed. "Maybe in a way or two, for the good. You were a teen; now you're a man. But I wouldn't call you *old* unless you go by what you've experienced. In that case, you're ancient." She offered a bemused smile, and Marek chuckled.

She stood up and pulled him out of the chair to his feet. Putting her hands on his shoulders, she studied his face. "You're the same Marek who got all muddy planting that tree in the backyard at our old house years ago. Who knows if that tree is still there? But I still have that wonderful memory, and you are here." She tugged him closer and whispered into his ear. "You'll always be the same wonderful Marek to me!"

They stood in an embrace for several minutes. Afterward, Marek took a last peek at the coin. Was it his imagination, or did it seem to have a bit more luster? He returned it to a safe spot in the drawer.

After they enjoyed a most welcome, hearty meal, their conversation turned away from the past and more to the future. His mother made a request.

"Marek, think of all your experiences outside of your homeland, Poland—they've all been horrible. Can you promise me you'll stay home for a while?"

Marek gazed into the distance as if he could see the future and the one thing there he couldn't deny. "I'm looking forward to sticking around for a long time, Mother. But my heart also yearns for this girl named Liddy. I'd love to tell you about her."

A gentle peace settled on him. They were up late.

Chapter 6

Late June meant more bugs. Keppler swatted one as he sat in the back of the truck with the railroad-track repair crew. He relished the trips away from the deplorable conditions at the prisoner-of-war camp, feeling fortunate Bernhard handpicked him for the team.

But today, they had got off to a very late start. The sun was lying low on the western horizon, large wisps of clouds caressing its golden face, promising a glorious sunset. *Must be an emergency.* It would soon be difficult to see without some sturdy lanterns.

"We're going to be doing something a bit different this evening," Bernhard declared. "Yes, you'll be using those shovels, but not for track repair." The truck slowed as they passed an entrance to a long road to a farmhouse, then continued farther up a hill and over the crest. The farmhouse was no longer in sight.

"Slow down," Bernhard shouted to the driver. "Turn in and pull up behind those trees."

A stand of tall pines stood in a row as if to greet them. There was no railroad track. The guard jumped out. But rather than bark out instructions, he listened intently, waiting for the next step from Bernhard.

"We're going to start digging up some potatoes. I want the back of that truck filled up. You'll be sitting on top on the way back, and I hope it's so high you'll almost be falling out."

Keppler sidled up to Bernhard and in a low voice asked, "Did you get permission from the farm owner?"

"Nah, we don't need to." He shoved his hands in his pockets.

"What?" Keppler twisted his neck around, and his gaze darted toward the field.

"Hey, man. It's everyone for himself in this postwar world. We'll sell what we can on the black market."

"Really?" He swallowed hard and scanned his surroundings. "A–and the guard will let you?" he stuttered, his mouth gaping open.

"Oh yeah. He wants to be a part of the deal." Bernhard's stare latched onto Keppler's eyes. "Now get to work!"

"I can't do this. It isn't right." Keppler crossed his arms, his shovel falling to the ground.

"Keppler, quit being so righteous." Bernhard shrugged. "If we don't do this, someone else will."

"I may have been on the wrong side of this war, but this sure isn't the kind of Germany I want to build. Let me fix railroad track, not steal potatoes."

"Everyone's gotta eat. You can help feed the hungry." Bernhard smiled as if proud.

"But at whose expense?" Keppler hissed, his voice louder, hands clenching. "I won't do it." Indeed, the latent stubbornness that had plagued him his entire life had boiled to the surface.

The guard, hearing the rising voices, stepped closer. Bernhard pointed to Keppler, lifted his shovel, and then shook his head. "He won't help."

The butt of the guard's rifle went whizzing by Keppler's head, fortunately missing it. Keppler picked up his shovel. He contributed very few potatoes to the bushels they gathered that evening.

⤶

In the kitchen, very early in the morning, Liddy watched Willy kneading bread dough. A low laugh rumbled out from her as she ruffled his hair. "My goodness, little brother, you've gotten good at this. You get up bright and early with such energy. Remember those days when I practically had to drag you out of bed? Now, you must be doing three times what I can do."

"Working fast keeps my mind off things… like losing Father." His shoulders drooped.

Ah, that she understood. She stepped aside and washed her hands to join him. "I know exactly how you feel. I'm so sorry about Father." Clutching the dishtowel, she stared at her hands, her chin twitching.

"Yeah, it's tough. Actually, though, Liddy, I owe it to you after you pulled me off my bus that had been bombed. You hurt your hand so bad protecting Keppler. Remember, you once thought you'd never knead again? Besides, my hands and fingers are now much stronger from my piano playing."

"I wish you could do more of your playing." She pulled a wad of dough out of a bowl and began to flatten it, pushing down hard on the center.

"Seems no one wants to come in to listen anymore. Everyone would rather just get their loaf of bread and scurry on their way."

"If Herr Keppler were around, he'd stay and listen." She began to hum a bar from one of his favorites, "Ave Maria."

"Yeah, I wonder if I'll ever hear back from the authorities about him."

"Oh, you sent the letter?" She furrowed her brow while dusting her hands with more flour. "How long ago was that?"

"Must be two months ago, now. I took it right to the post office. But who knows if letters ever get anywhere these days."

"I wish you had shown it to me. What did you say?"

"Trust me, Liddy. I really built him up. He meant a lot to me." Willy looked up at the wall clock. "Hey, we'd better get those risen loaves over there in the oven."

"Glad someone's watching the time. If you'll do that, I'm going to check on Mother."

Her bathrobe drawn tight, Renate was pulling the sheets from the sofa in the side room. She never made her way upstairs to the bedroom anymore. Perhaps she wanted to avoid memories of Klaus, but Liddy figured the trek upstairs was too hard on her mother's arthritis-filled body.

"Guten morgen, Mother. Hope you slept well." She hesitated, twisting a strand of hair around her finger. "Mother, I need to talk to you about something."

"Of course, dear. What is it?"

"Well, it's kind of personal." Liddy rubbed the back of her neck and cleared her throat. "Maybe you should sit back down."

"Oh dear, I hope it isn't what I fear." Her mother slumped to the sofa, shook her head, and pressed her fingers to her ears.

Liddy eased into a chair beside her. "That night of horror has come back to haunt us." She paused, swallowing hard. "I'm afraid I may be pregnant."

"Oh, Liddy, Liddy, my dear child. I pray to God it isn't so!"

"I've been sick in the mornings, more in the last few weeks. But don't worry, Mother. I can't go through with this." She chewed at the tip of a fingernail.

"What are you saying?" Pain filled her mother's watery gaze.

"The more I think about that night, the more it all bothers me so much. I just can't give birth to a Russian baby." She swallowed hard, then tore off a chunk of fingernail with her front teeth, avoiding her mother's gaze. "I need to terminate this pregnancy."

"Liddy! You know better—that's one of God's creations there. That baby wants to live just like any other baby."

"It just can't be God's will that I bear a Russian child. Especially after a Russian man violated me. But it's not just me that this is all about. A Russian killed Father—think about that." She spat the fingernail tip before spitting out words in frustration. "I despise those Russians!"

Mother pressed her lips tight and brought her hands up to massage her temples. "Liddy, your thinking is warped by all the misfortune you've endured. Please pray about it."

"I have been. I am not going to give birth to a Russian baby. Absolutely not."

"Liddy, my dear child. I have a confession to make." Her mother paused as though to collect her thoughts. "I'm embarrassed to admit it, but when I found out I was pregnant with you, I had similar feelings."

"What?!" Liddy sucked in a quick breath, her eyes widening as she leaned in. "What are you saying, Mother?"

"Let me explain. Back then, I went into a deep depression. We had just started the bakery. The last thing I wanted was a child to take care of."

Liddy's shoulders curled forward as she clutched at her stomach. "You're telling me you didn't want me?"

"Oh dear. It's so hard to explain. Fortunately, your father, bless his soul, brought me to my senses. He wrote this beautiful…"

Her mother buried her head in her hands, then shifted over on her side on the sofa. Liddy's gaze darted back and forth. She waited for her mother to continue, but nothing came.

Liddy bit her lower lip. After a moment, she heard a mumble she couldn't understand.

"Mother?"

Another mumble.

Liddy reached to help her mother sit up, but her eyes seemed glazed over. "Are you all right, Mother?" She moved her own head closer, this time detecting the word *weak*.

Something's wrong, dreadfully wrong. I just know it. I must get her help. Liddy held a hand to her own chest. She feared it was beginning to hyperventilate.

"Willy, Willy!" she screamed as loud as she had ever yelled out her brother's name. The boy soon charged into the room.

"Something's wrong with Mother." Emotion clogged her throat, choking her voice. "We've got to get her help right away." *Please, God, help me think.* These days an ambulance would take forever.

"I know… Herr Klein from church. He has a car. You remember where he lives, right?"

"Yeah, I think so. It's not far from here. Is Mother going to be okay?"

"I think so, if we hurry. Get on your bike and ride as fast as you can over there. Ask him to come here right away with his car. We've got to get Mother to the hospital. Hurry!"

~

Bernhard's crew had spent most of the day on rail repair. Keppler was pleased when that morning Bernhard let him diagnose exactly what had to be done. A far cry from analyzing a musical score, but Keppler felt confident. They had all worked hard—a flurry of shovels filled with dirt in constant motion. Now, as the sun set on the western horizon, they were off to another potato field. They dare not bring home the truck empty.

Keppler studied his hands as he sat with the others in the back of the open-air truck. Hands that once had trimmed nails and glided effortlessly across a black and white piano keyboard now were dirty and rough with jagged fingernails and callused fingertips. Hands that had once shown young Willy how to feel the emotion in "Ave Maria" now just ached, craving rest.

When they began digging for potatoes, he soon realized how hard it would be. To drive a tired body to work was one thing. To do it when the heart was not into it was quite another. Taking someone else's potatoes made it almost impossible. They returned to the camp with a very small load. And the guard's boss was surprised indeed. His eyes opened wide in disbelief as he summoned the guard.

"Who's responsible for this poor excuse for a load of potatoes?" The guard looked at Bernhard and without a word pointed to him.

"We had a very busy day repairing rail, sir," Bernhard said.

"That's no excuse." The boss moved to square his face up directly with Bernhard's, their eyes no more than six inches apart. Then his rifle butt smashed against Bernhard's face. With an "aaaagh," he bent over, blood dripping from his mouth. A blow to his stomach brought him to his knees.

Keppler could no longer stay silent. With chin raised high, he stepped forward.

"It is my fault, sir. I could not do this in good conscience and was a poor example for the others." He woke up the next morning, his head ringing, his lip split and puffed up, his eyes bruised and half shut, and no idea exactly what had happened next.

⌒

Marek tried many times to call the Mittendorf Bakery from Warsaw but could never get through. He didn't know if the service was still down or the bakery had closed. He hoped and prayed it was because Liddy was just too busy. Oh, how he wished he could see her. But at first, travel was restricted. That allowed him to recover from his ordeal, find a job, and earn enough for the long journey to Berlin. The newspaper in Warsaw was trying to get back on its feet. With a shortage of workers, they eventually would need a good press operator. Maybe then, his life would be somewhat back to normal. But without Liddy, it would be empty.

Chapter 7

Liddy sat by her mother's bed in the convalescent home hoping she would soon awake. The wall clock said three forty, but it sure seemed later than that. She surveyed the room with more than a dozen patients. Some were sleeping, others reading. Several men were moaning at the far end of the room, no doubt still recovering from war injuries. Away from the battlefield chaos, they probably didn't care about the general disorder around them, the dirt on the floor in the corners, or the antiseptic smell trying to cover up other more objectionable odors.

Three weeks had passed since her mother's stroke. When her afternoons were open, Liddy tried to visit, knowing not to expect an actual conversation. Her mother's eyelids finally opened.

"Oh, Mother. I hope you got a good nap. It's so noisy around here. It's a wonder anyone gets any sleep at all." Her mother mumbled something unintelligible in reply. "I am so tired myself." Liddy released a loud exhale.

"At least I'm done with the hard work. For weeks, they've had us women in cleanup crews after lunch," she went on. "I can barely lift some of the rubble we're trying to pick up out in the streets. Most of it is gone on our street, anyway."

"Hmmph," came her mother's response.

"But Willy and I are managing. He's become good at kneading the bread. We crank out dozens upon dozens of plain, old loaves each day. They're all gone by noon."

An admiring smile graced her mother's mouth. Liddy was learning to be content with such responses.

"I've been looking into what to do with this baby. That brutal, creepy Russian soldier, Ivan, keeps stopping by. I can't stand the sight of him, but somehow he persists in thinking we may have a future together. No way!"

Mother's brow became furrowed as she shook her head.

"I so miss Father. Why did God have to take such a good man so soon?" Her mother's eyes moistened. "We had such good talks."

How ironic, now I can't even have a conversation with my mother! They both remained silent.

"Then there's Marek." She took a deep breath, tingling her nostrils with the antiseptic scent lingering in the air. "I sure wish I knew what happened to him. Maybe he'll show up at our door one day like he did after Herr Keppler released him."

Thinking of the day Keppler got redeemed brought shivers up and down Liddy's spine. A gleam now formed in her mother's eyes.

"That reminds me. I almost forgot to tell you. Willy got a letter from the authorities. Keppler is at a prisoner-of-war camp not too far away. I don't know—is it possible to visit people at such places? Willy and I might just try to go see him some Sunday afternoon when we can get away from the bakery."

Her mother's face brightened, followed by a high-pitched squeal. Liddy wasn't sure exactly what that meant, but she imagined her mother said, "Wonderful."

⁓

Keppler sat on the ground and leaned back against the barbed wire fence. He had discovered a good spot where the barbs mostly pointed away, the wire giving his weary back a bit of needed support midday. He had already finished what meager lunch they were given. It indeed was a rare day when they were not out on rail-repair duty or potato harvesting.

Bernhard approached and sat down beside him, scratching what little light-brown hair remained atop his large head. His blue eyes sparkled as if trying to connect. "You surprised me, Keppler."

"What do you mean?" Keppler's eyebrows rose.

"You didn't have to step in to take all those blows from Dmitri." Bernhard smoothed the front of his tattered shirt.

"Might as well spread the pain around, though."

"That was no fun." Bernhard stuck his finger through a hole in his shirt, frowning at the disrepair. "Sure glad we got this day to rest. Maybe Dmitri could sense we needed it."

"I doubt it. I don't think compassion is in his dictionary. Must have been a scheduling thing. Anyway, it gives a person a moment to reflect." Keppler looked to the sky, his fingers laced behind his head.

"About what? Our future? I gotta believe we're so low in rank and valuable enough we're not gonna get tried for war crimes." Bernhard gave a confident nod.

"When I hear what all was done to some people, makes me feel not so bad about this life here," Keppler replied. "Maybe we deserve it. But I hope it doesn't last forever. I just regret blindly following the Führer."

"I still admire him." Bernhard picked up a stick and snapped it in two, rolling the pieces between his fingers. "If the whole world hadn't risen against us, we'd have won. Now we've got to deal with these wretched leftovers from the war."

"I so wanted Germany to rise up again. But I put country ahead of… everything else." Keppler's voice cracked with his last words.

"Nothing wrong with that in my book." Bernhard thrust his chin high.

"There's so much more that's important, I've come to believe." Shafts of sun streaming through billowy clouds appeared particularly beautiful, making him believe there could be a future, could be things like hope and beauty and music in this world.

"Like what?"

"Like faith in God and living your life with his moral compass."

"Oh, you believe in that? It's all a bunch of hooey. You can have every bit of it. You won't get anywhere preaching about that stuff around here."

"I can try," Keppler said in a steady, low-pitched voice. "Bonhoeffer was of great help to the prisoners at Tegel."

"Good luck with that." Bernhard drew his hand back and, with an "oomph," tossed the sticks as far as he could. "What is it about you people?" His nostrils flared. "Are you trying to feel like you're better than the rest of us?"

"No, I just want to spread the Good News. I also want to let God know I'm ready when He decides to use me to bless somebody else."

"Well, for starters, you can work on Waldo over there. See the short guy who still wears his army field cap?" Bernhard pointed across the courtyard. "I never saw anyone so down after the Führer committed suicide. He was actually crying."

"Sounds like he would be quite the challenge."

"I'll say. But stay away from his older brother. He's part of a different work group—you don't want to mess with him."

The ladder to the attic creaked under Liddy's weight. Years had no doubt passed since anyone else had put it to use. Once atop, she foraged through curtains of musty cobwebs until a stack of boxes loomed before her. Being organized had always been one of her mother's stronger suites. She must have saved that letter from her father. But which box? She brushed a layer of dust off several of them. Then one labeled 1925–30 caught her eye. She pulled out a stack of papers inside and thumbed through them.

Tears filled her eyes. These memories and written words were all she would get from now on from her father—spoken words no more. Likewise, her mother would never be the same—only a word here or there. A hollowness in her chest welled up as she fathomed how quickly history was slipping through her fingertips as each page flashed before her.

Yes, that made each word on each page before her precious. She must somehow haul the box downstairs and go through the written history more carefully.

Later that afternoon, she sat at the kitchen table—the letter she had so diligently searched for in front of her.

> Dear Renate,
> I am so sorry to hear your pregnancy is such unwelcome news and causing you such anxiety and depression. Childbirth is such a gift from God that we can so easily take it for granted. I do not blame

you if the realization of that has yet to register in your mind—let it take its own sweet time.

I'm convinced that, between the two of us, we have what it takes to raise two children at the same time—this brand-spanking-new bakery and a new child. By the way, I have a hunch it will be a girl whose first word will be *Mama*, even though I will have tried my hardest to teach her *Dada*.

Take your time to get your mind in the right place for all of this. Please, please be at peace. I'll be behind you and supporting you the whole way. (God will be as well.)

I love you more than you can imagine.

Your loving husband, Klaus.
Liddy rested her head on the table and wept.

In Warsaw, the factory superintendent stared back to size Marek up as they headed through a door from the office into the printing area. The hum of many presses cranking out newspapers was a welcome sound.

"You look awfully thin." The superintendent raised his voice above the din. "Are you sure you'd have the stamina to run one of these presses all day long?"

"Oh yeah." Confidence surged through Marek, lifting his lips. "I've experienced a lot throughout the war years. I can handle anything." They approached an idle printing press, off in a corner under dim lights.

"Well, this is it. Does it look familiar?"

"Wow!" was Marek's first reaction. "This one looks a lot like my Schatzi!"

"Schatzi?" The superintendent scrunched his eyebrows.

"I operated a press for Father Kolbe at his monastery until the Nazis shut us down. I nicknamed her Schatzi. It wasn't that far from us here in Warsaw. Schatzi and I had a thing going on. I could run her in my sleep." The hum of a nearby press brought his mind back to those days. He shook his head, recalling that day early in the war when he had made her appear ransacked so the Nazis would leave her alone. "This machine's beautiful."

"Tell me you can start right away, and you can run that beautiful thing tomorrow."

"Tomorrow?" Marek swallowed hard. "I was thinking of a couple weeks down the road."

"Oh no. I can't hold it open that long. I need someone now."

"But I have some unfinished business since the war ended. There's some people I must track down."

"Sorry, I can't wait." The man clenched his jaw. "I've got to offer this job to the first qualified person who comes through that door." He spun around to point at the entry.

Marek put his hand on the side of the machine, closed his eyes, and pondered. At last, he said, "Sorry, dear sister of Schatzi. I would have loved to get to know you."

⤴

Liddy made an effort to visit the convalescent home at least twice a week. Even though her mother was sometimes tuned out, Liddy was becoming more appreciative of their time together. She relished the opportunity to connect in at least some small way. A nod of her head, even just a twitch of her foot to some comment meant she was still a part of Liddy's life. And if she ever really kicked hard under the covers, Liddy had come to believe that meant, "Stay strong!"

Sometimes, when her mother was resting, Liddy visited the recuperating soldiers.

"So how come you never have any visitors?" she asked one day of a young man who rubbed whiskers that weren't much more than peach fuzz.

"Distance. My family is from Hamburg. What's left of them, that is—my mother and sister. I'm hoping to see them next month, though."

"So you're going to be here that long?"

He pulled down the covers revealing a bandaged leg half gone.

"I pray for your speedy recovery." Liddy lingered with her head bowed. She then gathered her things, kissed her sleeping mother on the cheek, and left for home. As she rounded the corner to the bakery, a bright light glowed at the end of the block.

Chapter 8

Liddy ran toward the bright light. Billows of black smoke streamed toward her, stinging her eyes. A light from a fire truck flashed repeatedly. Her mouth fell open.

"It's the bakery!" she screamed out. "Help, my dear God!" Her heart raced. Faster and more determined, she ran, her breathing heavy. "Where's Willy? Where's Willy?"

As she approached the front of the building, two men with spray hoses were working to extinguish the flames. Emerging from a cloud of smoke, Willy ran to her, clutched her waist, and buried his head into her chest.

"Oh, Liddy. Oh, Liddy!" seemed to be all he could say as he shook uncontrollably.

"Are you all right, Willy?" She grasped his head and looked him straight in the eye. "Tell me you're okay."

"I think so. But our bakery—just look at it!" They watched arm in arm as the men tried to put out the stubborn flames.

Twenty minutes later, they could only stand before the smoldering mess. A crowd of onlookers lingered in the distance. The remains of the Mittendorf Bakery sign that so often drew glances of admiration from her father swung above them.

"Father would be so disappointed. We worked so hard to make a go of it. He must be in heaven looking down with tears in his eyes." She wept her own tears, mouthing, "I'm so sorry, Father...."

"Well, it sure wasn't our fault." Willy crossed his arms, his quivering chin jutting. "It was those stupid Russians."

"What? What are you saying?"

"That weird guy who keeps trying to be friends with you. What's his name? Ivan? He and his soldier pal were here. They went into the kitchen while I was sweeping in the front room. Before I knew it, they'd left in a hurry. The flames soon came jumping through the kitchen door."

"Oh, dear God, help." She kept shaking her head back and forth. "What are we going to do? Just what are we going to do?" she repeated, her voice trailing off with no hope for a quick answer. She stood still and stared into the distance, then dropped to a knee in prayer.

"I just didn't know where else to go, Anna. We're so grateful." Standing in Anna's apartment, Liddy pulled Willy close, and the three of them hugged.

"We all have to make do." Anna swiped her dark bangs to the side. "I owe it to you. Think of all the time your family put me up last year when I was so fearful of being nabbed by the Gestapo. Not to mention the risk you took harboring a Jew."

"Well, we were happy to take you in. Now we all have to get on with our lives without our men. Sorry, Willy." Liddy patted his back and winked. "But you're still getting there."

He smiled.

"I'm still shocked about your father." Anna moved to retrieve some glasses from the cupboard. "Apple juice?" she asked, and they both nodded. She poured and handed them their drinks. "I can see *my* father disappearing," she continued with a sniffle, "but I never would have thought we'd lose Klaus right at the end. He was such a wonderful man."

Liddy teared up and edged away to go stare out the window. Willy slumped into a chair.

"It's been a dreadful couple of months, topping off all those dreadful years of war," she summed up. "I just don't know where God has been all this time."

"Well, He chose to keep us alive, and we have this roof over our heads." Anna pointed to the ceiling. "We can't complain."

"Maybe I'd be better off if I hadn't been spared. Think about it. I lose Marek, I lose my father to war and mother to a stroke, and the family bakery burns down. Wouldn't you be mad at God?"

"No doubt, you've gone through a lot, Liddy. At this point, though, we've got to think about putting our lives back together." Anna took a swallow of juice. "There's no rush. As they say, 'one day at a time.' " She closed her eyes and tipped her head back.

"You're fortunate you can find that peace."

"You'll get there." Anna glanced at her watch. "Say, I was throwing together something for dinner before you came. Let me add to it, and we can all sit down together. Willy, you're good at slicing onion and chopping carrots, aren't you?" He sat speechless in his chair.

"Just kidding. I'm sure your sister can help with the cutting."

After dinner, Liddy stood at the window again as darkness began to descend upon them. "I know you say, Anna, that God has helped us all through this, but I don't know what to think anymore." She twirled around and approached Anna as she was rinsing some dishes at the sink. In a soft voice, she said, "You haven't even heard the whole story...." She drew in a deep breath and released it.

Anna pushed the faucet handle down hard. "What? There's more?" She turned and laid a gentle hand on Liddy's shoulder. "Tell me."

But Liddy winced, stepped back, and shook her head.

"Yes, you must. Haven't we known each other for a long time, now? Who else on earth is going to help you?" She reached to hug Liddy and whispered into her ear, "We're here to support one another. You have to talk to me and let me help."

Liddy glanced at Willy, hesitating. She then clasped Anna's hand and pulled her into the bedroom, closing the door behind her. She walked to the mirror above the low dresser and frowned as she examined her body, her shoulders drooping. Tears began to trickle down her face. She turned sideways. "Don't you notice anything different about me?" she whimpered.

"No." Anna finally shrugged, meeting her eyes again. "What?"

"Can't you see there's a baby in there?"

"Oh, Liddy! What happened?"

"Those despicable Russians!" She lowered her voice in fear of Willy listening. "The night they came storming into East Berlin back in April." Anna could piece together the rest.

"Oh, Liddy," Anna repeated, tears welling in her big brown eyes as she grasped Liddy's hands and squeezed. "When is the baby due?"

"End of January. But the story gets even worse—the father has kept coming back to the bakery. Believe it or not, he thinks we could have a relationship."

"Oh, you poor girl!" Anna cringed and turned away, shaking her head.

"If that isn't enough, I'm convinced he burned down the bakery. He got mad because I wouldn't have anything to do with him. After everything we've done to keep it going these past years. I hate the Russians. They killed my father, they destroyed the bakery, and they violated me. There's no way I can give birth to a Russian baby."

"Those are a lot of pretty strong words coming from you." Anna seemed to have a hitch in her breath as she brought her hand to her chest. "Liddy, Liddy. Think this through. That's a child of God in you. Besides, it's too late to terminate this pregnancy."

Liddy stiffened. "Why would I even want to bring another child into this awful world? Especially a Russian child?"

"Please… Don't do anything rash. Promise me you'll keep praying about it. Who else knows about the baby?"

"My mother does, but I haven't had the heart to tell Willy." She ran a hand through her hair, pulling at clumps of it as if she could make the pain come from somewhere else.

"What about your father's parents? See what they have to say. You could probably stay with them for a while. Not that you aren't welcome here." A long exhale streamed from Anna's mouth.

"Yes, that could be a possibility. Oma and *Grossvater*. I need to check up on them now, anyway. But I've still got to get back to the bakery to see what personal items can be salvaged. For the time being, is it okay if we store them here?"

"Of course. My home is your home." Anna stepped forward to hug Liddy.

※

Liddy pulled the four-wheeled wagon with Willy to the bakery's front door. That Anna's neighbor had such a thing and was willing to loan it to them was a godsend.

She slowed as they rounded the corner. The bakery's charred black structure loomed in the distance. Now, more than a blight to the neighborhood, it was a blight on her heart, and the pain was lingering there ever so long. "Willy," she mouthed, her head taking over. "We're going to have to limit it to what fits in the wagon. At least for now. Anna doesn't have a lot of storage room."

He tipped his head, a wise look coloring those blue eyes beneath shaggy hair needing a cut. "Things like pictures rather than bread pans, right?"

When had he grown up? She nodded, unspeaking.

As they surveyed the remains of the first floor, her heart sank. Most of the wood structure was charred black, the brick outer walls just a shell. The prized picture of her grandparents on the wall, without the glass that had broken during an air raid, was destroyed. Not much of anything could be salvaged.

"My piano!" Willy moaned as he gazed from a distance. "Just look at it—all that crud on it!"

"Come, let's check it out," Liddy encouraged him.

"No, I can't." He stopped in his tracks, his head turning to the side.

"We must face up to reality, young man, even if it's painful." She grabbed his hand and edged him forward. At first resisting, he then relented. Approaching the piano, he placed his fingers softly on the soot-covered keys, holding them there as his eyes darted back up to Liddy. He finally dared press down. It sounded like birds making their last chirps. So sad. His shoulders slumped.

A solitary tear streaked the soot on his face before he turned away.

Liddy explored the ruined structure further, finding Marek's old rucksack. She pulled out his mother's keepsake brooch and his father's compass. Remembering the picnic when Marek had shared their importance, she held them tightly in her hand and breathed a prayer for him.

Upstairs, they rounded up some small pictures and clothes, but scant else. She also located a set of her mother's favorite earrings, along with some of her journals. In their parents' room, she retrieved her father's keychain and a bundle of Bonhoeffer's letters bound by a rubber band deep in a desk drawer.

She lifted the top, and read a highlighted paragraph.

It is only by living completely in this world that one learns to have faith. By this-worldliness, I mean living unreservedly in life's duties, problems, successes, and failures. In so doing, we throw ourselves completely into the arms of God.

She could not imagine being immersed in life more so than now.

She clutched all of the keepsakes close to her breast as Willy pulled the wagon back to Anna's abode. The smell of charred wood soon faded, but not the visions of the remnants of their former lives. Neither said a word. What was there to say?

⸺

Flat on his back, Keppler eased his eyes open. Through the blur, he could not recognize the person on a chair beside him, but the pain throughout his body was very real.

"Where am I?" he mumbled, his gaze darting. "Who are you?"

"My name is Marthe."

"Well, I don't want some middle-aged woman with messy hair doting over me. I can get myself up." He tried sitting up but fell right back with an exasperated *hrumpf*. "So, you didn't tell me where I am. No more messing around. Be straight with me."

"You're in one of the guard's tents."

"Guard's tent? Are you crazy?" His body stiffened as he tried to raise his head again. "What am I doing here? Get me out before they discover us!"

"Don't worry. The guard won't be back for some time. I keep track. He's off with some work crew. Just relax now. We need to get you cleaned up." She squeezed a cloth from a pan of water and wiped his forehead. It stung.

"What's happened to me? I ache all over."

"Waldo's brother beat you up."

Waldo's brother? "I don't even know him."

"I didn't either. But I was nearby when he clobbered you. He said something about not wanting you messing with his brother's mind. Some reference to Bible stories." She sighed. "I'm a believer, too. I asked one of the other fellows to help carry you in here."

"Ah, so that's what this is about. Waldo seemed to be showing some interest." After another struggle, Keppler sat up and, hard as it was, tried to project a smile. He scanned the tent, seeing little more than a bed, side table, and trunk.

"So, I'm sorry for being so gruff earlier. That's my old self seeping out. Gets me frustrated. I hope the scowl on my face has begun to soften."

She nodded with a chuckle.

"But tell me." He raised his eyebrows. "Why is somebody like *you* in a place like this?"

"The Russians consider me an enemy, too. I'm a nurse, but my name appeared in some pretty bold anti-Communist editorials in the newspaper just before they took over. They tracked me down."

"You'd be much more valuable in some hospital."

"But I am glad I can help the folks in the POW camp." Her confident smile widened her face, revealing bright white teeth. Light-brown hair, pulled back into a ponytail, framed her blue eyes and fair complexion.

"Needless to say, I'm glad you're here, too." He snickered.

"So, what's your name?" After squeezing some salve from a tube, she dabbed it into a scrape on his cheek.

"Keppler. I used to patrol the streets of Berlin until I got pushed out to the frontlines in January. The Russians captured me." He shrugged. The rest was obvious.

"Well, keep doing what you're doing. Remember, Jesus said it would never be easy. Nobody said you have to be a preacher. Use the tools you have and be an example for others."

He nodded, followed by a satisfied smile. "You're right… you're right. Say, thanks for watching after me today. You can call me Conrad." He released a heavy exhale. "I'd feel better if I got up and out of here. If I were anything like Paul and Silas, I'd be singing to God with praises. They'd been beaten with rods and thrown into prison." He banged his hand atop the side table. "Well, anyway, I hope to see you around. Maybe we can share some notes."

"Indeed. I would welcome that. I don't think I'll be going anywhere soon." She gave his knee an affectionate pat and left.

༄

Liddy sat with Pastor Reinhold in his church office. He straightened a pile of papers on his desk, then looked up, appearing to give her his full attention.

"So where will you go now?" He clasped his hands, his pointer fingers pressed to his thin lips, and leaned back in his chair.

"For now, Willy and I are staying with a friend, but I'm going to check into moving in with my grandparents in Bavaria."

"We will certainly miss you." He stared directly into her eyes and shook his head. Liddy had an idea of what he would say next. "Well, God has sorely tried many of us during this awful war, but you, Liddy, and your family have had more than your share. To think of your parents, that attack on you, and now the bakery." He spread his hands wide as though to indicate her helplessness.

"Sometimes I just don't understand God, pastor." A mighty frown dragged her face down.

"We only have to look to the Bible to see other people supremely challenged by God. Just take the suffering of Job, for example." He bowed his head.

"I know, pastor. But why? I've been a faithful servant all these years. And remember, I even organized that clothing drive here at church." She paused. "What kind of reward is this?" She pointed to her belly. "I can't stand the thought of giving birth to a Russian baby!"

"Remember, you have a child of God there. Psalm 139 says that baby was 'knit together' by God in your womb—that it was 'fearfully and wonderfully made.' All his days were 'ordained' and 'written in His book.' Read that over and over again until it sinks in and continue to pray about it."

Liddy's stomach churned. She was familiar with the passage, but it just wasn't registering. Her fingers twitched on her restless knee. "I wish I could get my heart around it." She bit her lower lip, and her gaze darted around the room. "Why won't God help me with this?"

"He will. Be patient." He thumped his fingers on the desk. "It just takes time."

"But I'm running out of time." The words squeaked out from her desperately dry throat.

"Maybe that's His answer. Did you ever think of it that way?" He stood up to wish her goodbye. "Pray, my dear Liddy, and know that God said, 'Turn to me in your hour of need, and I will love you with a love that will last forever.'"

"He encouraged me to keep the baby with lots of fine words," Liddy exclaimed to her mother the following day. "But, of course, no surprise with that."

Her mother's visage brightened, and a peaceful smile graced her lips. Liddy just knew that engaging with her about her visit with Pastor Reinhold would make her day.

"But to be honest with you…" Liddy fiddled with a ring her mother had given her, tight on her finger. "I'm still struggling." As her mother's expression flattened, Liddy wondered how she could make it worse by telling her about the family bakery burning down. Even though she could blame it on that nasty father of her baby? Save that for another day. At least she could share that she'd be gone for a while.

"I'm going to take Willy with me to Munich to see Oma and Grossvater." Her mother's eyes widened. "He's been anxious to spend some time with them."

"So you won't see us for a week or so. But I'm sure you'll do just fine." After visiting a bit longer, she bent over and gave her mother a goodbye kiss on the forehead.

Chapter 9

Early on a Friday morning, her rucksack on her back, Liddy wove her way through the myriad of travelers at the bus station. It was teeming with people, no doubt, because many of the trains were subject to limited service. She glanced back often to make sure Willy was keeping up. His heavy rucksack slowed him down. Soon she was standing in line with him to purchase tickets. He was studying a map, his brow furrowed.

"Where did you get that map?"

"Marek gave it to me." He held his chin high.

"I should have known." She patted Willy on the shoulder. Fond memories of Marek on a bike trip with her, his map sticking out of his pocket as he raced ahead, flashed into her mind.

"I've been studying this," Willy chimed in. "You know, if we go out of our way a bit, we could stop to try to find Herr Keppler in the prisoner-of-war camp." He gave a confident flick of his index finger onto the map.

"Really? How much out of the way is it?"

"Only three or four hours." His eyebrows lifted.

"That's a long time, Willy. Besides, what would our chances be of actually finding him?" She pressed her lips together. "Pretty slim, I would guess."

"But this might be our only chance. They could move him any time or even try him for war crimes. Then what?"

"I don't think so." Liddy ran a hand through her hair. "Oma and Grossvater are expecting us."

"But we could still make it by late tomorrow. Please? It would mean so much to me."

She tilted her head from side to side, then looked up to find the station wall clock. "I don't know, Willy. It would amount to an extra half day." She unfastened the flap of his rucksack, peered inside out of curiosity, and then reclosed it. "Well, okay, I must admit I'd like to see him, too. Let's give it a try. But I'm expecting you to navigate."

"Wahoo!"

Marek could wait no longer. Since attempts to contact Liddy had been unsuccessful, now that he was back to full health, he was anxious to travel again. He'd surprise her in person. Who knew? Maybe he could resurrect his old job in the kitchen? No doubt, those signature *M* loaves had long missed his artistic talents. Klaus and Renate would welcome him with open arms. He, of course, would envelop Liddy in his own arms. And they would make up for time lost.

With the train from Warsaw to Berlin now up and running, he could talk his way past anyone trying to restrict his travel. He could hardly believe he'd be making the same trip as the one a few years back when he was fleeing after the Germans invaded Poland. At that time the train was packed. He doubted that would be the case today.

The bells from the nearby church steeple rang loud, tolling in nine a.m. Time to catch his train.

Many empty seats stared back at him inside the gray-toned car, only about two-thirds full. Crumpled newspapers and magazines shoved haphazardly into back pockets of the seats along with empty disposable cups left it far from neat. Marek took an aisle seat, next to a young lady making copious notes in a notebook. Not until the train had pulled out of the station did she acknowledge his presence with a cheerful smile.

"Hello. How far are you going?" she asked with probing eyes.

"Berlin." He offered a welcoming nod.

She brushed her dark bangs off her forehead. "Don't tell me—you have family there, right?"

"Not really. A cousin, Anna. I'm also trying to check up on some other folks I used to work for there. They owned a bakery."

"I see. I've got a long trek to Munich, where I grew up and my father has a hardware store. It barely survived the war, and I'm going to help him get it up and running again." She held her chin high.

"Yeah, operating a small business was especially tough the last few years. As if bombings and air raids weren't enough." Marek's mind wandered to Liddy, who had done the same thing to help her father at the beginning of the war.

"You can say that again. Now it's a real challenge to find men, or anyone with hardware knowledge, to help run the place." She scratched the side of her cheek.

"Well, if I were going to Munich, maybe I could help you out. But sorry, not going that far." A nervous light laugh followed.

"If things don't work out, keep us in mind. Here, I'll leave you my name and address. Who knows, maybe we could get together for some other fun times. It's about time we all broke out from the yoke of a terrible war." She winked as Marek put the note in his back pocket.

Liddy and Willy approached the barbed-wire fence of the prisoner-of-war camp. Ominous shadows from the nearby trees seemed to be crowding out what few shafts of light made it to that part of the courtyard. The stench of humans living in close quarters under terrible conditions clogged the air.

Willy raced ahead a dozen paces, clutched the wire fence to peer in, then looped back to be close to her. He repeated that several times. "How are we possibly going to find Herr Keppler? Look at all those people in there! There must be thousands."

"I wonder where the entrance is." Liddy lifted onto tiptoe, craning her neck.

Frowning, Willy readjusted how the heavy rucksack hung on his back. "Do you suppose there's a place where visitors need to go?"

"I don't think so. They weren't thinking about that when they built this place. They're trying to keep people from getting out, rather than getting in." Liddy yelled out at someone inside near the fence. "Excuse me. Would you happen to know a Conrad Keppler?"

The fellow just ignored her and walked away with a scowl. Liddy shook her head, but then reminded herself this was not a welcoming place.

Willy started to shout out his name. "Herr Keppler, Herr Keppler!"

That's my Willy. She pinched the top of his shoulders, a grin broadening across her face. It wasn't long before she joined in as well, and together they walked along the barbed wire calling out his name. After about fifteen minutes, a heavyset man sprinted to the fence from afar.

"I know Keppler." As he studied them from head to toe, amusement crinkled his cheeks. He swept a hand over his thinning hair. "Let me go find him for you. It may take a while."

When the well-spoken man strolled away, Liddy and Willy smiled at each other and slumped to the ground, their backs resting against the wire fence.

"After all this time." Willy plucked a blade of grass, rubbed it between his fingers, and then peeled one side off. "Could it be we've found him?"

"To think he's had to live in such a dump." She smoothed her travel-creased skirt and closed her jacket loosely over the rounding of her stomach. "What a change for a music professor—someone who fancies the finer things in life."

"Willy! Liddy!" a familiar voice called out. "I can't believe it."

Liddy scrambled to her feet. Willy's lips stretched wide as he hopped up beside her.

Keppler put the palms of both his hands up to the fence, the tips of his fingers poking through the openings of the barbed wire. He connected first with Willy, then Liddy. A rare smile spread across his face.

"I can feel the energy in those fingertips." He laughed. "The energy of a piano player if I ever saw one!"

Tears dribbled down from Willy's eyes, and Liddy reached to wipe them away.

"I never thought this could happen," she said. "Herr Keppler, so how are you?" It seemed a strange question considering his circumstances, but she wanted to know deep down how he felt.

"I'm managing to survive. It's not exactly a four-star hotel." He chuckled while peering back. "But God looks after me." He released a gratifying sigh, and a bemused smile widened on his face. "When I get bored, they send me out to repair railroad track or dig graves."

"My, that's an odd combination of tasks for a music professor." She released a loud sigh and waved a hand. "So much has happened." *How I despise the slight whimper in my voice! We've come to bring him cheer not depression.*

"How goes the bakery?" His eyes sparkled as if it brought back fond memories.

Liddy was delayed in her response. "Well, I'm afraid the bakery is... history." She ducked her chin and struggled to get the words out as her lips twitched uncontrollably. "The Russians burned it down."

"Oh no. What a crying shame." He turned his head to the side and rubbed his face as though scrubbing at the disgusted expression overtaking it.

"The piano went with it," Willy chimed in, his voice breaking up.

"I'm so sorry." Keppler gritted his teeth with a scowl. "So, do you have a decent place to live?"

"For a short time, we stayed with Marek's cousin, Anna. But we're actually on our way to our grandparents in Munich."

"Ah, that's nice. And your parents?"

Unable to respond, Liddy studied her callused hands. She'd lost so much. "Father was a war casualty, and Mother had a stroke. She–she's in a facility." Tears trickled down her cheeks.

"Oh, my dear. May God help us!" He banged his hand loudly against the fence. "I'm so sorry, Liddy. Klaus gone? As you say, much has indeed happened."

"I have so wanted to be strong. I just can't believe what God has put us through." Her chin trembled.

"A lot—no doubt about that." He released a long exhale and closed his eyes as if to gather his own emotions.

"Herr Keppler, I'm ashamed to say it, but I'm so mad at God right now."

Keppler jolted and stared into her eyes, extending the tips of his fingers again through the barbed wire. His fingertips were so warm. She lingered to maintain contact.

"That's not all," she whispered.

"Don't tell me—can there be something else?"

"I might as well come right out and say it. I'm pregnant." Her gaze darted to Willy, whose eyes bulged. "It all happened the night the Russians took over Berlin."

"That despicable Red Army." Keppler's grip tightened on the fence, his head wagging in slow motion back and forth.

"This is news for Willy, too." She snugged her arm around his shoulder. "I've got to do something in a hurry.

I'm not going to raise a Russian after everything they've done."

"Liddy! Surely that must mean you're going to put it up for adoption, right? That's God's child you've got there."

Liddy just kept staring into his eyes.

"Remember," Keppler continued, "what you once convinced me? You need to forgive and forget. I had lost my brother and my wife. *You* reconnected me with my God. Your forgiving me for shipping Marek off to a camp shook me to the core. I realized I must forgive, too."

"And who did you forgive?"

"God." Keppler's eyes sparkled, and peace settled across his face.

The single word, the single *truth*, zinged through her soul. She stiffened. "I'm just not ready," she released the words in a whisper. "I can't stop thinking of Marek, too. Wondering about him has been a daily ritual, that's for sure."

"Now that the camps have been liberated, maybe he'll resurface."

"I can only pray that will happen."

"Pray to the God you still don't trust?" he mouthed softly. The glint of his eye seemed to be casting an uncanny wisdom!

"Oh, Herr Keppler, I don't know what to do." She took a step back, stroked her arms, and kicked at the dirt.

"You must pray for both Marek and that baby. Stop being so mad at God that your prayers come off as hollow."

"Hollow?" Her head tipped up, her eyes letting his eyes capture them again.

"You give it only lip service. All that anger keeps you from really trying to connect. Think about it."

She rubbed her forehead, muttering, "I don't know.... Maybe you're right." She took a deep breath.

"Promise me you'll truly pray for both Marek and that baby. And I mean pray—in earnest."

Liddy's cheeks burned and her chest tightened. She stared down, unable to meet his eyes. A moment later, she murmured "I'll try" and released a heavy sigh as her gaze gravitated back up to his.

"Not good enough," Keppler snapped, his cheekbones rising.

She paused and pursed her lips. She'd forgotten what it was like to fight with him. "No. Okay, I will. I absolutely will!" Her chin stiffened.

"Keppler," the call came from behind them. "We've got to talk about tomorrow's work plans."

"I've got to go. Seeing you both has made my day!" A rare shaft of sunlight settled on his face.

"Thank you for your words of encouragement." Liddy's lips twisted. "Payback, indeed, I should say. Who would have ever thought the tables would be reversed?"

"Wait. Just a minute," Willy interrupted. He pulled a small Bible from his front pant pocket. "I got this for my last birthday but figured you could use it." He pushed it through a small opening in the fence.

"I am ever so grateful, Willy." Keppler held the Bible up, and his lips flattened.

"But what will happen to you, Herr Keppler?" Liddy stepped forward, closing her fingers around a smooth length of the barbed wire.

"Don't worry about me. Everything is going to be all right." For a few seconds, he stared into her eyes, then her brother's before backing off. "Just let God help us get through it all."

With a satisfied sigh, he turned and left, the sound of his humming *Ave Maria* fading in the distance.

Chapter 10

A battle of war and peace was playing out in Liddy's mind. She felt so at peace finally sitting in her grandparents' living room, the dark brown sofa with sculpted wooden legs under her. Yet merely reciting the events of the last year brought the war to the forefront. Sitting safely on a soft sofa in the Munich apartment was so restful, but talking about the Russian invasion and the bakery that was no more was so vexing. The war was indeed over. Shouldn't that be enough to lift her spirits?

"So I'm hoping, dear Oma, that you are okay with Willy and me staying here until we can sort things out." She leaned in to get a good read on their reactions.

"Of course, Liddy. We wouldn't have it any other way. You'll have to sleep on the sofa and Willy on some blankets on the floor until we can locate a cot, or at least an air mattress." She took a sip from her cup of tea. "We can certainly make room in these trying times."

"That should be fine, Oma." Liddy glanced over toward Willy to validate that he'd bought into the plan.

"I had such a grand time here that summer before Father talked me into coming back to the bakery."

"So, what took you so long to get here on this trip?" Oma picked up a plate of cookies and passed it to Willy in the next seat.

"Well, everything still seems to be running much slower. Then we also stopped to see Herr Keppler in a POW camp." She shielded her eyes from the bright light coming through a window.

"Keppler? You wrote about him, a Nazi officer who helped Willy learn to play the piano?"

Grossvater, quiet to this point, interjected a "Hummph."

"He had changed, Grossvater," Liddy was quick to add, flipping her hair back.

"Yes," Willy confirmed. "He really helped me. I learned so much so fast." He took a chomp out of his cookie, some small pieces falling to his lap unnoticed.

"He reconnected with his faith and set Marek free." Liddy twisted her hands in her lap, still feeling his grip on her, his charging her to reconnect with *her* faith.

"Oh yes, now I remember." Oma stood up to go pull a window shade, then turned to her husband, repeating the news about Keppler, making sure he had heard.

"So, Grossvater," Liddy interrupted, "Did you find out anything more about Father's body? You were going to check into it further?"

"Well, they confirmed he was buried on the battlefield, but no explanation as to why they took so long to notify us."

Oma brought her hand to her eyes, no doubt hoping to stop the tears that were about to flow as she thought about her son.

Seeing that, Liddy started weeping. Oma rushed to her bedroom.

"It's just not fair," she asserted upon her return with a clean handkerchief.

"What's that?" asked Grossvater.

"You very well know, Gunter. Losing two sons to war!"

"I know, I know." Liddy threw her arms out. "Two fine men like Klaus and Friedrich. I miss Father so much! Our talks together were something I'll never forget." She dabbed at her eyes with a handkerchief. "I know Willy here misses his father, as well."

Willy nodded but remained quiet.

"And how about your dear mother, Liddy?" Oma asked. "What a terrible situation that turned out to be."

"She's getting along. Can't talk much—that's how badly the stroke affected her. I tried to get over to see her a couple times a week. At least I can feel connected, even though it's just a bit."

"Such a shame." Oma sniffled and released a heavy sigh. "So, what about Marek? What do you suppose has happened to him?"

"I trust he is somewhere. But only God knows. Some days I can't stop thinking about him." She looked wistfully off into the distance as silence took over the room.

Several minutes later, Liddy reengaged. Just as she had relayed to her mother and Keppler, she went on to reveal that a baby was due near the end of January and how she had been devastated by the thought of bringing a Russian child into this world.

⌇

Marek may as well have been in some foreign land, not Berlin. The old Anhalter train station, hollowed out by multiple bombings, was just a shell of its former self. Even though several months had passed since Hitler had occupied a bunker in this once stately city, the remnants of the last days of the war were everywhere. Though the streets were mostly cleared of rubble, the buildings still displayed the holes from which that rubble came.

He walked the long trek to the Pankow district, envious of those on bikes like the one he had used to ride at dizzying speeds through what once was a bustling metropolis.

As he came upon the street along which the Mittendorf Bakery stood, the sun appeared to be brighter than he remembered for this time of day. Gone were the shadows cast by some of the buildings. Then reality slapped him square in the face. The bakery had burned down! He spun away from the revolting sight, his hand over his eyes. He let out a cry. Where was Liddy? Had she been in the fire? What about Willy, Klaus, and Renate? Though most of the bakery still stood, it was deathly quiet. Gone was any sign of the lifeblood that once inhabited it, not to mention the bustle they brought to the fine place.

He hailed a passerby. "Excuse me. Do you know anything about the family that lived here?"

"Sorry. I do not," came the curt reply with a shrug.

Marek paced back and forth, his gaze darting. He brought a shaky hand to his forehead. *Should I go in? What might I find?* Wracked with indecision, he collapsed, his rear end hitting the curb with a thud, his hands at each side of his head. "Why, Lord, why?" he found himself muttering. Gone was his plan to return to his life of kneading bread with Liddy. She loved his *M* signature loaves, didn't she? Would she ever see one again? Would he ever see *her* again?

At last, he summoned the courage to venture inside. The unnerving feeling of looking at familiar things now charred black haunted him. Eventually, he located and bemoaned the loss of things burned almost beyond recognition—the apron he used to wear each day, his favorite electric mixer, and the rucksack containing his family keepsakes. The rucksack fell apart. Had his keepsakes—his mother's brooch and father's compass survived? Gone.

A hollowness seized his gut. He fell to his knees, and his hand searched through the satchel contents again. A sudden noise far off to the right brought him back to his feet.

"Who goes there? Wait!" he yelled out. A short dark figure with a bag in hand leapt by him headed to the front door. Marek lunged for him but tripped, the full force of his body rolling into a charred support post. The weakened structural member gave way, and plaster and boards from the ceiling above came tumbling down on his head, giving him but a few seconds to catch a glimpse through a cloud of soot of a boy escaping out the front door. Then all went dark.

The darkness was replaced by another as seemingly hours later Marek regained consciousness and surveyed the pitch-black room. As he struggled to get up from under some timbers, the appearance of two small arms startled him by helping to lift the beams off him.

"Who are you?" Marek asked.

"I'm Rolf. I just had to come back to see if you were all right."

"You were the one I saw run out? What were you doing here?" He remained sitting on the floor, brushing the debris and dust off himself with his hands.

"Well, like a lot of other people"—in the darkness, Rolf swept a shock of light brown hair away from his eyes and tilted up a proud chin—"I was looking for things that might be worth something."

"So you're a scavenger, huh?" Marek cocked his head to the side. "Maybe I should call you 'Rat' instead of Rolf. How old are you, anyway?"

"I'm twelve. I'm just doing what everybody else does."

"Well, I happen to know the good people you're stealing from. In fact, I used to work here." Marek paused in thought. "And I may even be able to find a flashlight."

He got up and made his way to a kitchen drawer. "Wait right there, and I'll be back in a second." He returned, flashlight in hand.

The dim light bounced off charred walls, finally settling on the short lad's face as his dark-brown eyes squinted above hollow cheeks, then refocused on the floor where he sat.

Marek, still feeling dizzy, sat down beside him. "You're awfully young to be scavenging through burned-out bakeries. I do appreciate your coming back to check on me, though. But tell me, I did see you with a bag. What sort of things were you hauling out of here?"

"Oh, nothing much." His eyes remained focused on the floor. "I know the family, too. Willy was a friend of mine."

"Is that right? I've been away for a while. Do you know what's happened to Willy and the rest of the family?"

The boy shook his head without another word.

"So how do you feel about ransacking the property of a good friend? You can't feel too good about that?"

"Willy wouldn't care about silverware." As his scrawny shoulders shrugged, Rolf stared off into the distance.

"Ah, so you took silverware after all. What do you think your father would say about that?"

"I don't have a father anymore."

Those disheartening words sank in slowly. Marek had wanted to try standing, but with those words, he remained on his knees, his butt resting on his heels.

"So sorry to hear that." He pressed comfort into his tone. "Was he a war casualty?"

"Well, I need to get going." The boy scrambled to his feet.

"I can imagine so. How late is it, anyway?" Marek looked at his wrist for the time, forgetting that a watch was no longer there. "Your mother's probably wondering where you're at."

"Actually, I'm the one wondering where she's at. Haven't seen her in days."

Marek's aching body remained motionless. "So you've got no one at home?" He cast a long stare off into the distance, not expecting an answer. "I've got an idea. A cousin of mine lives not too far away. Hopefully, she'll be able to take us both in for a few days."

Marek tried standing up on both feet, but wobbled. He gripped the boy's shoulder, and Rolf put his arm behind his back to offer additional support.

"Well..." Marek let out a long shuddery breath. "Should we see how far we can get like this?"

As they headed out the door, the imposing figure of a man lurked by a distant streetlamp, its light casting long shadows. They eased down the sidewalk along the street. After a block, Marek asked Rolf, "Can you look back to see if that fellow is following us? My neck is still stiff."

After a quick turn of his head, Rolf replied, "Yeah, he seems to be. By the looks of him, he's a Russian soldier."

Two blocks later, Marek, still supported by Rolf, asked him to check again.

Rolf turned. "Gee, that creepy soldier is still following us."

"Well, I've had enough. I'm going to confront him."

"Careful, Marek. The Russians control everything around here now."

"I know." They turned and started back while the soldier continued to approach, none of them slowing down. Soon Marek's face and the soldier's were a mere eight inches apart. The soldier towered over him.

Marek blurted out, "Why are you following us?"

"I noticed some suspicious activity around that burned-out bakery. What were you doing there this time of night?"

Marek's shoulders arched. "What if I were to ask you what were you doing surveilling it at this time of night?"

"Enough of your lip, or I'll throw you behind bars."

"Well, let me tell you. I know the owners—the Mittendorf family—that used to live there. In fact, I used to work there. I'll bet you're just trying to find Liddy. I've got a better chance of finding her than you do."

"We'll see. She's going to regret hiding from me." The disdain on his face matched his tone. "Come along. I'm taking you in." He reached for Marek's arm.

But Rolf yelled "No way!" and barreled his head into the soldier's stomach.

The Russian stepped back, gasping for breath, but grabbed a healthy hunk of Rolf's hair and tossed him aside like a bag of potatoes. "Stay out of this, kid!"

Rolf continued to tumble to the sidewalk.

"You're going to need me to find Liddy, soldier. For sure, she's not in that bakery. Now leave us alone." Marek extended an arm to help Rolf up. The two of them continued down the block arm in arm as the soldier remained standing in place.

"You should have seen his face." Rolf squeezed his arm tighter around Marek. "I would say it was glaring."

⸺

Marek reunited with his cousin, Anna, giving her a long, heartfelt hug. Was such a hug a reflection of their time apart? Or deep down was it from a fear of a world changed so drastically, it was beyond recognition?

"So what's happened to you, Marek?" she gasped, surveying him from head to foot.

"Had a little accident at the Mittendorf's burned-out bakery. Man, what a shame. Is that ever a depressing place now. Fortunately, my new friend, Rolf, was around to help me," he added, introducing him. He soon was thrilled to hear better news about Liddy and Willy but distressed when Anna could not provide their exact whereabouts. Klaus and Renate's fates made him wince and cover his face with his hands.

"I'll not stop until I find Liddy," he declared. "If you'll have me, I'd love to stay with you here in Berlin as my home base. And then Rolf, too, until we can find one of his relatives." Marek explained the situation with the boy's deceased father and missing mother.

"Of course, you are both welcome to stay." She hurried to the window. "Truth be told, Marek..." She lifted an edge of the curtain, then slapped it shut again and jumped away a little. "The presence of a man in the house is most welcome." Her gaze strayed to the window, the curtain battened down as if she expected an air raid. "A Russian soldier... has come back. I've seen him at that corner before." She swept her hand to the left. "Makes me nervous."

"Yeah, he's no secret to us. He's back this time because he followed us from the bakery! We had an encounter with him down on the street. You should have seen young Rolf here step up."

The boy shuffled his feet as a flush crept along his cheeks.

"He first showed up the day Liddy came after the bakery burned down. And he... he *looks* toward this place all the time. Maybe it's my imagination, but..." She shrugged and rubbed her arms as if chasing away chills.

He stepped forward and reached to lift the curtain to get another look, but she stilled his hand and shook her head. "Let's try to get him out of our minds, and focus on something else."

From Marek's perspective, that meant finding a job. He had no idea how the war impacted the job market, but figured one thing was for sure—there were fewer men around. That afternoon, he checked with the newspaper where he had previously worked part-time. A press operator position was open. He grabbed it.

One day, figuring that Liddy most likely was living at an unknown location with her grandparents, Marek had an idea. He recalled the research he had done for Liddy to find a picture of the Mittendorf Restaurant opened many years ago by her grandfather and subsequently closed. Could he find in the newspaper archives a story about its closure that might reveal the next steps for the owner?

"Eureka," he had exclaimed upon coming across the story after several weeks of searching. But, much to his chagrin, there was no mention of the next steps or location for Grossvater Mittendorf.

Keppler sat in the back of the open-air truck with the work crew as they made their way back to camp. Next to him were Bernhard, Waldo, and several other men. The passing landscape was beginning to look more barren, many of the leaves having already fallen. Five months since the end of the war. But plenty of soldiers who had lingered with severe injuries could not overcome them, finally losing their battles for survival. After a hard day of work, Keppler tried to rub the dirt off his hands, but it was particularly stubborn.

"Of all the things we do, this is one that gets me thinking," he said loud enough so most of the others could hear him.

"Grave digging?" Waldo chimed in. "It's pretty simple to me. You put the body in the hole, cover it up, and all is done." He pushed down on his worn-out Nazi Army field cap with a stroke of finality.

"Then what?" Keppler lifted his head, meeting the short man's gaze. "Is that the end for most of them? How many of those souls are going on to everlasting life?"

"You're not going to get started on that stuff, are you?" Bernhard briskly brushed away some leaves that had settled in his lap. "Please, let's not have preaching here in the back of this truck."

"Well, do you guys ever think about things like this? When it's your turn, what's going to happen? After death, we are meant to renew. Think about nature." Keppler gestured to their surroundings. "All those leaves out there have died, but in the spring, there will be new buds—new life. You've got to move out of the past and move forward. Take you, Waldo. You're still hung up on Hitler. We now know the man was evil. Sometimes you have to admit you made a mistake and move on."

Waldo just shook his head.

"Jesus told a story of a vineyard owner and his fig tree. For three years, he had it planted in prime soil, but it never bore fruit. They gave it one more year, taking special care to fertilize it. Still nothing. 'Cut it down,' said the vineyard owner. Sometimes you have to step back and make sure your life is on the right path. I rejoice in knowing I have a future life with Jesus that will be everlasting."

"At this age, I'm pretty set in my ways." Waldo tilted his head back, clasped his hands behind his neck, and scowled at the overcast sky.

"It's never too late. Jesus would welcome you with open arms. There's another story about a prodigal son who, after a period of wild living, came back home. His father was so happy his son had decided to change his ways, he threw him a party, much to the chagrin of the other brother. The father was so pleased because the lost son was now found."

The truck pulled through the POW camp gate. Gusts of wind whipped some leaves on the ground into an eddy. While the others got out, Waldo lingered in the back of the truck. Keppler hoped the ideas in their minds were stirring as well. And though those leaves were meant to die, to be replaced by new in the spring, would these souls ever understand they were meant to live on?

~

Marek sat with Rolf on the sofa in Anna's apartment. A Sunday afternoon seemed to be a good time to delve further into the young lad's background.

"I hope you don't mind my asking, but what was your mother doing the day she disappeared?"

"She went grocery shopping. The store near us was running out of food. She went to a bigger one on the south side of town."

"How long has it been?"

Rolf's eyes bounced back and forth. "It's been several weeks now."

Marek frowned, biting his lip. "How did she get there?"

"She has this really nice bike. It's got a big basket on the front handlebars."

"So much going on," Marek muttered. "Bicycles can be prized possessions. I've even heard of people getting shot over them." Marek grimaced. "Oh, sorry. Didn't mean to alarm you. But sometimes we have to face up to reality."

Rolf squirmed in his seat, at last responding. "That's all right. I know you've gone an even longer time without Liddy. How long does it go back to?" His eyebrows raised in anticipation.

"The fall of '44." Marek gazed longingly out the window.

"For a younger guy like me, that would be a long, long time."

"I'm not that much older than you, ya know. Speaking of time, you mentioned you have a cousin in Munich. How long has it been since you've seen him?"

"Must be four or five years. I hardly remember him." Rolf sat quietly. Finally, he rubbed a hand over his eyes. "I do have to confess, Marek, I haven't been straight with you. It's been more than a few months that my mother's been missing."

Marek's chest hitched. "Wow, Rolf. So sorry to hear that!" He draped a comforting arm around the boy's shoulders. "Before coming here, how were you able to get by?"

Rolf lifted his chin again, shaking that shock of light-brown hair away from his eyes. The kid needed a haircut. "I was trading what I scavenged for ration cards."

"Must have been some harrowing months without parents."

"Still is, what with everything up in the air."

"We're long overdue checking more with the authorities. Tomorrow after I get off work, let's head over to the police station to see if they have any updated information."

⸺

Monday afternoon, Marek felt queasy about entering the police station. Yes, it was all different people there now.

But the building was the same, and the memories from a few short years back cascaded through his mind—Herr Keppler locking him up, then later escorting him out to freedom—albeit temporary.

He and Rolf approached the receptionist. "We're here to check about a missing person," Marek said.

The older lady with graying hair set her pencil down. "A pretty common request these days. Let me pull records out of the file. What's the name?"

"Bertha Werner. I'm her son," came Rolf's shaky response.

The lady thumbed through some files in the cabinet, finally pulling one out. "I show we sent a letter out to the residence about six weeks ago. That was after being unable to round anyone up there."

"Really?" Marek leaned closer to the counter. "Do you have a copy for us to see?"

When the lady handed it over to him, Marek rested his other hand on Rolf's shoulder. "May I read it, Rolf?"

The boy nodded with a worried frown.

After a few seconds of reading, Marek dropped his hand with the letter to his thigh. "Let's go sit down a minute." He motioned for Rolf to take a seat in the waiting area, and he sat down beside him, making a deeper read of the letter.

"I'm so, so sorry, Rolf." He reached to pat the boy's leg. "First your father, now your mother. This letter says she was found shot in an alley. They tried stopping in to see you, but no one was home. You must have missed this letter. I don't know what to say other than how devastated I am to see you have to go through this now too."

As Rolf's face erupted in tears, Marek stood and reached to give him a hug—one that lasted more than a few minutes.

Chapter 11

As the Christmas season approached, Liddy battled mixed feelings. Yes, she indeed could feel joy celebrating the birth of the Savior child. But for the first time, it would be without Father, and even Mother, who was so far away, present in her thoughts only. From the sofa, she stared off into the distance as the others settled into living room chairs one Sunday afternoon. The smell of apple cider wafted through the room as Oma had a pan warming on the front burner. Grossvater worked on a puzzle on the coffee table.

"I'm not planning on spending much time at the Christmas Market." Oma bustled to the kitchen. "But you can bet I'll be making some lebkuchen."

"That's such a tradition, I don't know what I'd do without that tasty morsel," Grossvater said. He held up two puzzle pieces to check for fit.

"I can already taste it." Willy scooted forward to the edge of his chair. "But do we have to wait until Weihnachten to put up a tree?"

"Yes, that has always been our tradition in this household." Grossvater nestled those two pieces into a corner of the puzzle, then glanced up, his glasses slipping down his nose.

Shifting in her seat to tuck her feet under her, Liddy sighed. "But Oma said the tradition of a goose would go by the wayside—too expensive."

"We haven't had one of those since before the war." Oma looked toward the kitchen. "I'd better go check on that cider."

"You'd think now that the war's been over for months, things would get back to normal." Willy scooped up some nuts from a dish on the table beside him. "When will that ever happen?"

"Unfortunately, it takes a long time to recover from such a devastating period in our history." Liddy reached for a handful from the dish he passed her way. Hm. Not too salty.

"It took a long time after the First World War, Willy." Grossvater flipped over several upside-down pieces, then pushed them away with a huff. "I'm just hoping the Church can see a bigger role in bringing the country back." He tapped a pointer finger on the table. "I see where they admitted they could have done more years ago."

"I missed that," Liddy said. "How so?"

"Back in October, they came out with what was called the 'Stuttgart Declaration of Guilt'." He put a puzzle piece down and gazed up. "I'm trying to recall the four things they admitted they should have done more years ago. Let me think." He scratched the top of his head, his fingers penetrating furrows between a few stubbles of short gray hair. "The first was to profess our beliefs more courageously, then pray more faithfully. Another was behave more joyously. And what was the last one? Oh, yeah—love more intensely."

"Well, I know Dietrich Bonhoeffer tried to do his part." Liddy nodded her head. "Unfortunately, he did not survive the war to lead us on." Her mouth turned down.

"Now, it's up to us." Oma returned with a tray of cider and cups. "If we could just get our own house in order first, we could focus on the rest."

"As for me, I hope to be able to contribute to our financial coffers," Liddy interjected. "As soon as I have this baby, I'm going to try to teach at a school."

"Oh, Liddy. I can't tell you how happy I was when you decided to have your baby." Oma made the rounds pouring cups full.

"You wouldn't believe how hard I prayed to God, Oma. Herr Keppler said I must pray in *earnest*. Giving birth was the clear answer I kept getting from God."

"What have you got? Six more weeks?" She settled back into a chair and cocked her head toward Liddy.

"Yeah, that time will go by fast." Liddy leaned back, at ease.

"Teaching," Grossvater repeated, seemingly anxious to change the subject. "So, what was that you said about teaching?"

"I've always dreamed of doing so. There are great teacher shortages because many were disqualified for ties to the Nazis. Willy can attest to how bad it is."

"Yeah, I'm still getting used to being in a class that seems like almost a hundred kids with the one teacher. Sometimes it gets pretty noisy."

"But before I get a job, I need to see if I can find a place for Mother in Munich. I've got to believe conditions are less crowded here than in Berlin. Medical care now is just awful there. I think she could handle the move. She's a tough soul."

"Great idea," Oma said. "Then our family would be all together—what's left of us, that is." After a quiet reflection, Oma broke the silence. "Liddy, speaking of family, where does that leave your new baby? Gunter probably wouldn't be all that excited about it." She looked his way, then moved forward in her chair, her hand on one knee. "But we could manage to take care of the little one while you go off to teach."

"I've prayed hard about it all, Oma. I've decided I'm going to find a good Christian family to raise the child." A deep, satisfied breath followed.

The coals in front of Keppler glowed, providing little light, but more importantly, the heat was keeping them all warm on this mid-January night. Beside him, to his left, was Waldo, ever close by the last few weeks. To his right was Bernhard, trying to scribble on a piece of paper in the dim light.

"Aren't you glad we were able to *requisition* that coal, if you know what I mean?" Bernhard snickered.

"You know where I stand on ill-gotten potatoes, coal, and any other scarce commodity, my friend. I'd rather we found some we didn't have to steal." Keppler looked across the yard at the other fires surrounded by people rubbing their hands together.

A shiver traced his spine. "Is it me, or does it seem like our numbers are getting fewer?"

"Oh, fewer, without a doubt." Bernhard's pen stilled. "It only makes sense if you think of all the grave digging we've had to do lately. What a waste of coal."

"No, I mean besides that. Are they letting people out?"

"Reassigned, I should say." He poked at the coals with a stick. "As a matter of fact…" He chewed on his lower lip. "I'm working on that now."

"What do you mean?" Keppler massaged the back of his neck as the coals sputtered.

"Russia," came Bernhard's one-word response.

"What?" Keppler narrowed his eyes.

"The Russians are figuring out they could use a number of us rebuilding their own country. They're shipping lots of people off, along with machinery, even. You were one of them."

"Come again?" He fidgeted with a button on his shirt.

"See this list here. Your name was on it, but I've changed it." He handed the list over to Keppler, who leaned closer to the coals to make it out.

"I see my name here, but it's crossed out."

"And whose name is put in its place?" Bernhard asked while Keppler squinted back down at the paper.

"I see. What does that mean?" Keppler stammered.

"It means I'm going, and you're not."

"To Russia?" Keppler's eyes bulged.

"Yes." Bernhard flashed a toothy smile. "You know I'm a man of adventure."

"Sure you are, but who made that change?"

"I did." He ran his fingers through his short gray hair.

"This is big news. Why would you do that?" Keppler rubbed his hands together.

"Two reasons. First of all, you've got family, and I don't."

"Family?" he blurted, his head shaking back and forth.

"Yeah. You couldn't hide it from me." Bernhard leaned in. "I saw you interacting with your daughter and son through that barbed-wire fence. The looks in all of your eyes—such love."

Keppler burst out with a subdued laugh. "They weren't my children, Bernhard. Only friends from a bakery

I frequented in Berlin. I don't have a family anymore. My wife is gone, and the first terrible war took my dear brother."

"They sure seemed like family, the way they came to see you and were so glad I could go find you." Bernhard rubbed his chin and paused. "Well, then… there's another big reason. I love my country. More than anything, I want to see it recover. You know that. The country desperately needs people like you to build it back up. Once the Russians realize what they've got, they'll set you free. Even people like Waldo over there."

"But that could have been you!" Keppler stood up, turned away, and then looked back.

"Well, it takes a special person with skill and character. I'm not there yet." Bernhard sighed heavily. "I'm working on it, but I'm just not where you are at." He avoided eye contact.

"Why, thank you, Bernhard. I don't know what else to say." Keppler's voice quivered slightly as he reached out to shake his friend's hand.

"But you've got to promise me something else."

"What?"

"Now that you'll be the lead man on the railway repairs, don't mess them up." Bernhard chuckled.

"You've got it." A slow smile formed across Keppler's face. He was thinking not only about his new responsibilities but also about Bernhard's new sacrificial view of himself. And the Mittendorf children.

⁓

Oma put a hand on his restless knee. "Your fidgeting won't make it happen any sooner," she said as Willy sat together with her and Grossvater in the maternity ward waiting room.

"I get tired of all this waiting around. How much longer do you suppose it will take?" He sprang from his chair and moved to gaze out the window at a late-January afternoon snowfall. A few adults were walking along the sidewalk, but no kids. They were all stuck in school. Being here for a special event like today's made him unique. He cocked his head.

"We just can't say, grandson. It could be minutes; it might be hours. All we know is that Liddy's labor has started."

Grossvater stood and joined him at the window. A deep breath shook the tall man's thin frame.

Hugging his arms about himself, Willy faced Oma. "Liddy doesn't seem to be too excited about having this baby, does she?"

"Well, is it any wonder?" came Oma's quick retort. "Once she hears something uttered from the baby's sweet mouth, that will all change."

"We'll see." *Had Grossvater just shuddered?*

"Does she have names picked out?" Willy ran his hand along the heat register. *Seems kind of weird that she hasn't talked about at least a few. I would have, if I had anything to do with it.*

"Not yet," Oma huffed.

After they'd waited about thirty more minutes, a nurse came with the news that a baby boy weighing three kilos had been born.

"Is that big or small?" Willy asked as he moved close to Oma.

"About average." She tucked an arm around his shoulder, drawing him close to her.

"Can we go in to see them?" He breathed in her scent. *Had she dusted herself with baby powder in anticipation of the visit to the hospital?*

"In a few minutes. They're moving her to another room." She gave him a tight squeeze.

"You two go in. I–I'll stay here," Grossvater stammered.

"Why, Gunter, aren't you anxious to see the baby?"

I'll bet Grossvater doesn't like the sound of babies' crying.

Grossvater turned to gaze out the window again. "I'll wait here." He shot an uneasy glance back at her.

Grossvater is acting kind of weird.

Oma walked over to face Grossvater. She raised both of her hands to his shoulders and looked him directly in the eye. "Something's wrong, Gunter. I can sense it."

"I'll be okay. Don't let me upset you." He rubbed his arm, chasing shivers, but Willy knew they had nothing to do with the cold.

"You're not ready to see that baby, are you?"

"Shhh… not in front of Willy." Grossvater's gaze darted to him.

Yep, for sure something else is going on—it isn't just the baby's crying that's bothering Grossvater. And they didn't want me to know about it.

"Oh, Gunter. Please don't do this now," she whispered.

"You're the one who's pushing it." The words came past pressed lips, the way they did when he tried not to scold Willy for talking about Oma's age in front of other adults.

"Gunter, this is *Liddy's* baby. Think. This is *your granddaughter's baby*," she stressed each word.

Grossvater gave a half-hearted shrug and stepped toward the door. "I'll go in. But don't expect me to hold it and go all 'gaga' over it."

Oma just shook her head and muttered as they walked out of the room. *Seems kind of strange that Grossvater was calling the baby an "it" when they all now knew Liddy's baby was a "boy."* Now that he was the boy's uncle, he at least knew that!

Chapter 12

Although the shortest month, February dragged on particularly long for Keppler. They were doing less away from the POW camp, and being sedentary during the cold days meant they relied more on fires made from the scarce coal. But at least he could focus on friendships within the camp.

"Where did you get all this, Conrad?" Marthe asked him as she dug into a bag of bandages and other medical supplies he had laid before her.

"I know this fellow who works at the hospital. We got together while I was out on repair duty last week. But I can assure you, they are not ill-gotten."

"This will certainly come in handy around here. I hope I don't need these bandages again because Waldo's brother is feeling irritable."

"Couldn't agree with you more." He laughed. Then he leaned over to cross medical supplies off a list of needed items. "You know, Marthe, I would be remiss if I didn't say it's a wonderful thing you're doing around here, tending to the medical needs of all these prisoners." He reached for her hand and gave it a squeeze.

She flashed him back a knowing grin. "There are still too many people here. I would have thought by now they'd have released more who are not considered a threat." She pinched her lips together.

"Especially harmless people like you who could be helping so much on the outside. I mean, really, you write a nasty editorial and end up here? Maybe I need to write something nice about you to someone else?" he mused with a smile.

"I'm only happy to be of help while I'm here. But it's oh so different from what I came from."

"How's that?" He focused his gaze on her face.

"My family was pretty wealthy—that's until the Great Depression. I'm used to living in conditions a bit nicer than what we have here."

"Anything would be better than this." Just saying those words brought a reminder of the stench they dealt with each day.

"I've grown used to it. You know, Conrad, over the years, I've come to appreciate the words of Lilias Trotter."

"Who's she?" He tilted his head to the side.

"She was a nineteenth-century missionary to Algeria whose writings I've come across. Lilias said that love's strength stands in love's sacrifice."

"Yes, I can believe that." He nodded.

"But then she ties that into suffering."

"How's that?" His forehead wrinkled.

"She said, 'And he who suffers most has most to give.'" Her eyes were wide and probing.

"Beautiful, just beautiful. How true. We all have had a lot to give." He paused in thought. "For my benefit, I should say, Marthe, I'd be happy to have you stay here a while."

"I'm liking the Kohler family more and more with each visit," Liddy announced at the dinner table one early-March evening. "The baby seems to be very comfortable with them."

"Well, that's good to hear." Oma swallowed a bite, then continued. "So does this mean they are the ones?"

"I think so. I pray they are. I'm checking into some additional information, but everything looks good to this point. You know, this makes the third time I've been there."

"We'll have to go with you that day that you finally hand the baby over," her grossvater piped in. He soaked up some gravy on his plate with a piece of bread. "Where did you say they lived?"

"Ingolstadt. It's only about an hour away." She put her fork down and peeked up as she felt her face tightening.

"That would be nice of you, but you wouldn't have to come with me. I can handle it myself." She bit her inner cheek as she shuffled her feet under the table.

"Well, it's going to be hard for you, Liddy." He drew in a deep breath. "We better come along to make sure you go through with it."

"Gunter!" Oma put down her fork, her eyes blazing. "Don't put it like that. Liddy is perfectly capable of handling this."

"I'm only speaking the truth. This will be one of the hardest days of her life. We'd better go with her."

Liddy frowned and pushed her peas to the other side of the plate. She knew deep down Grossvater was right—it would be really hard. But she was a woman now, a mother. Perfectly capable of handling things like an adult. At least that's what she hoped and prayed.

"Excuse me." Liddy pushed her chair from the table and headed to the bathroom. An uncontrollable whimper escaped before she could pull herself back together. She dabbed at the corners of her eyes. "Thank you, Oma, for the dinner."

Marek had not attended Liddy's church in Berlin very often in the past, mostly because it was located so far from his uncle's and cousin's apartment where he had lived farther west in the city.

Now, as he sat listening to the pastor's sermon, the words were not registering. His mind drifted to the day he had helped Liddy in the church basement, lifting boxes of sorted clothing. The welcoming look on her face when he had shown up unexpectedly forever lingered in his heart.

He shifted in the pew, anxious to talk after the service to other parishioners about her possible whereabouts.

"I suspect she's living with her grandparents down in Bavaria somewhere, but I wouldn't know exactly where," said one friendly lady. "Check with Frau Bauer over there. Maybe she knows."

Unfortunately, Frau Bauer did not know what city they lived in, either.

"That's such a shame about her parents and the bakery," Frau Bauer lamented. "God has tested her."

"I'll say," Marek replied. "Losing both your parents is so devastating."

"Well, at least her mother is partially here."

"Partially here?" he gasped. "Wait. Is she still alive? I didn't know that." He wiped his sweaty palms on his pants. "What do you mean?"

"A stroke victim. Can hardly utter a word."

"What? I thought she had died of a stroke. Bad assumption. Where is she?" He rocked on his feet.

"No, the stroke wasn't final. She's packed into a convalescent facility with a load of other people."

"Where? I need to see her!" His chin jutted out.

"Well, strange you should ask. Some of us at church here were planning a visit to see all sorts of people there this afternoon. Cheer them up, that sort of thing."

"Count me in. I'd love to join you." He grabbed Frau Bauer's shoulders and gave the startled woman a big kiss on her cheek.

⁓

Late in the afternoon, Keppler stood with Waldo gazing down at a plot of ground next to some other tombstones. Keppler handed Waldo a piece of paper with some information about another site. "Check, this one out, too. Will you?"

Several minutes later, Waldo's shout echoed across the graveyard. "This one looks ready to go, as well."

Once Waldo had rejoined him, Keppler said, "But let's do one at a time, digging together. I think it will seem like it's going faster."

"Okay." Waldo nodded while giving his shovel a twirl.

"Waldo, I hope you don't mind if I sing while I dig. You know, to honor those being buried tomorrow. Remember—I've got a musical background."

"Go ahead. I trust you have a decent voice." Waldo chuckled. "What are you going to sing?"

"An old German hymn—'Stille, Mein Wille'. The words were written by Catharine von Schlegel, and the music is from Sibelius's *Findlandia*. But I only remember the first and last verses."

"Suit yourself." He shrugged.

Their shovels pierced the sleep of the fallow ground, and they began in earnest to remove the dirt. The melodic sound of Keppler's voice carried throughout the graveyard.

"Be still, my soul; the Lord is on thy side;
Bear patiently the cross of grief or pain;
Leave to thy God to order and provide;
In every change He faithful will remain.
Be still, my soul; thy best, thy heavenly Friend.
Through thorny ways leads to a joyful end.

"Be still, my soul; the hour is hastening on
When we shall be forever with the Lord,
When disappointment, grief, and fear are gone,
Sorrow forgot, love's purest joys restored.
Be still, my soul; when change and tears are past,
All safe and blessed we shall meet at last."

Afterward, Waldo removed his old Army field cap, took one last look, and threw it into one of the open pits. He jumped in and covered it with dirt. Once he had climbed back out, Keppler put his arm around Waldo's shoulder as together they walked back to the truck, hopeful that he had cast aside the old and was finally open to the new.

Chapter 13

Marek let the members of Liddy's church pave the way. He had never been to a convalescent home like this, where a dozen patients occupied one room. Upon inhaling the antiseptic odor, his nostrils flared, putting him on the defensive. As he stood in the background, he admired the chitchat, the smiles on peoples' faces, and the exchange of pleasantries. Except for Frau Mittendorf, with whom there was little exchange as others mostly just nodded politely. Her eyes finally met his at a distance, and her face brightened. He stepped forward to greet her, lifting her hand gently, his other hand cupped over the top of hers as if a protective shield.

"Frau Mittendorf, I'm so sorry about what has happened to you. Never would I have imagined seeing you like this under these circumstances." He scanned her bed from head to toe. "I'd rather be carrying you over my shoulder headed down into the cellar during the most awful of air raids. Remember when we did that?" He answered the question for her. "Of course, you do!" He tried to force a smile. "Coping with war was easier than living with its after-effects—at least in some ways."

Sitting up in bed, her lips widening ever so slightly, Renate bobbed her head up and down. Oh, how some sort of communication was better than none! Marek pulled a chair closer to the bed and sat down.

"Of course, I've missed Liddy terribly." His eyes started to burn. "I was hoping you could tell me where she's at. Wait… I mean I know you can't tell me. But maybe… maybe you could write it down." He looked around for paper and pencil. A fellow patient a mere two feet away overheard and offered her letter paper and pen with a book to write on.

"Oh, thank you so much." Marek grasped the writing items and placed them in Renate's lap. Her hand shook as she held the pen. Then arthritis made writing doubly frustrating. She was having a difficult time pushing down hard enough to make the letters show up. After several frustrating minutes, he put his hand over hers and gave a gentle squeeze of appreciation. He eased the paper from her, then held it up to his eyes. The letters spelling *Munich* became evident.

"Good, good!" He sprang to his feet, excited. "Do you have an address?"

Renate sat in thought, then shook her head slightly back and forth.

"Oh, that's a shame." He slumped back into the chair next to the bed. He had come up with very few details, but it was a start. "Is there anything else you can relay to me?" This time she was able to write a date: March 8.

"A date—what's the significance of that?"

Renate became anxious and tried to blurt something out. But the mumbled word was unintelligible.

Marek tapped his restless fingers on the note and surveyed the room, hoping for some inspiration. But then a surge of guilt filled him. He had made this all about him and Liddy.

"So, are you doing okay, Frau Mittendorf?" He smiled. A blank stare that probably camouflaged her real wellbeing was all he could detect. He scowled at the floor and shifted in his chair. *Dare I try one more time?* "Does the date mean something, Frau Mittendorf? Can you write it? Let's try again."

She reached for the paper and book, but her hand collapsed, the heavy book dragging it immediately to the bed.

"I know you're getting tired, my dear Renate. Can we try one more time? I'll hold it all for you. Just once more?" After several minutes, she had managed to write another word: *GONE*.

"Gone? What does that mean? Will Liddy be gone? Is that why you wrote the date?" Did he detect a nod?

"Will Liddy be gone from Munich by March 8? Is that what you're trying to tell me?"

Renate's head slumped back into her pillow, and her eyes closed.

∽

In the POW camp, Keppler leaned over to pick up a brown banana peel. Today, he had been assigned cleanup duty. Although it wasn't the most pleasant job, he felt good to eliminate at least some of the sources of the foul odor. And now, as he deposited the peel into a bag, Marthe began a slow trot toward him, a big grin stretching her face.

"Good news, Conrad! I've just been notified I get out of this place in three months."

Losing Marthe's personality, even more than her medical expertise, would be a real disappointment, but it was best for her.

Keppler felt his gaping mouth turn into a smile. "That is wonderful news, Marthe. I'll bet you can hardly wait. I will miss you—that's for sure."

"They're probably happy to have one less mouth to feed."

"I suppose so." He dropped his bag. "More food for the rest of us." He opened his arms wide to offer a big congratulatory hug, and she obliged. "What did they tell you?"

She pulled some paperwork out of her pocket. "I haven't read beyond the first paragraph. Let's see." She perused the notice. "It says that, based on a doctor's recommendation and a critical need on the outside, my release has been approved. I can't imagine what doctor would have done that."

"Let me think...." He tapped a finger to his lip in staccato. "I know of one." He couldn't hide his smirk.

"What? Wait... It was you! I never realized you were a doctor."

"Well, not a medical one. But I do have a PhD in music, so that qualifies me to be called a doctor. I signed the recommendation as Dr. Conrad Keppler."

"Well, I love your diagnosis, Dr. Keppler." A warm laugh rippled over her lips. "Thank you so much for petitioning on my behalf!"

"You're welcome. For someone like you, it was easy to do. I'm sure some medical staff would love to have you." As a piece of paper blew by, he wished he'd been more adept at retrieving it, but in reality, that wasn't a skill he would need for long. "Actually, I've got some good news, too."

"No!" She gave him a playful jab on the shoulder. "Why didn't you say something earlier?"

His smile widened. "Didn't want to take away from your joy."

"Don't tell me you're also getting out!" Her fingers came up to her parted lips.

"Yeah, but I've got to wait six months. They're doing some restructuring of the transportation department. That, along with the petition of a family friend, has helped."

"We'll certainly have to get together when we're both free. I'd love to hear more about your music background and your friends." She released a shallow sigh as her face brightened.

He gazed warmly into her eyes. "I would look forward to that, as well," came his bubbly voice.

⁓

Getting to Munich before March 8 meant Marek had to leave Berlin the next day. He wasn't sure how he would locate Liddy once there, other than to go through the Mittendorf listings in the telephone book.

He had suggested Rolf come with him since the lad had a cousin there he might be able to stay with for a while. Marek viewed it as an opportunity to connect with the one who now was without parents.

A steady rain early the morning of departure slowed them down. No matter—they would get to the train station in time. Once there, the dismal sight of the war-ravaged place depressed him.

"Here, you can take the window seat, Rolf. I'll take the aisle. But confirm for me first. Are we on the right train?

It's been such a crazy last few days, they all look the same to me."

"And you're supposed to be showing me the way?" The boy chuckled. "We're still going to Munich, right? Where you still hope to find Liddy Mittendorf?"

"Yes, indeed."

"Well, I can prove we're going in the right direction." He pulled out something from his pocket. "According to this compass, we're pointed southwest."

Marek did a double take. The compass looked like the one he had kept as a keepsake from his father. He reached for it and tumbled it in his hand. "Do you remember where you got this?"

Rolf shrugged. "I spotted it on the ground outside the bakery."

The wheels below squealed as the train eased out of the station.

"It looks familiar. I'm pretty sure we can trust it." He pressed his lips together. "Be sure to take good care of it. We'll talk about it some more later. So, how have things been going for you? We've been fortunate to have someone to stay with like Anna."

"Fine. I appreciate her taking me in until I can find somebody else." Rolf slid it back in his pocket, then wiggled a bit on his seat and swept his bangs away from his forehead as if he'd gotten used to moving them away from his eyes. At least, Anna had cut the kid's hair. "I'm just now getting used to my parents being gone. I used to have nightmares about the day the soldier came and told my mother and me about Dad."

"Yeah, nightmares. I know what you mean. I can relate to that." He took in a deep breath, followed by a ragged exhale. "I can't stop dreaming about a death march to a ship in the Baltic."

Rolf cocked his head and eyed him. "A death march?"

"Yeah, believe it or not, thousands of people were marched to the sea and were drowned or shot there. I was one of the lucky ones to survive." Marek raked his fingers through his hair, disbelief uncoiling inside him again.

"Wow!" For the first time that day, some color filled Rolf's face.

"So, are you pretty much done with the nightmares?" Marek looked him straight in the eye.

"Not completely, but I've learned to accept things." Rolf turned to stare out the window at the passing landscape. "My mother had to teach me to let go of things that happened in the past that we have no control over. She always said there is nothing we can do about what is history. We have to accept things and look to the future."

The kid had a wise mother. But… "You have every right to continue to grieve the loss of your father and now your mother. It's just plain hard to fathom it all. Don't feel like you have to rush it." Marek looked at the bag of chips he'd brought with them, thinking he'd offer some, but no, it was too soon in their trip.

The locomotive whistle blew long and loud as the train pulled into a station at the next town.

◦

Marek opened his eyes and took a glance at his newfound wristwatch, one that had belonged to his uncle. "Rolf, what's happening?" It sure didn't seem like he'd been out for two hours. At least there were no drawn-out nightmares.

"You should have woken me up. But I guess that's to be expected," he mumbled, "when you've been up the whole night before."

"Thinking about Liddy?"

"Yep." Marek glanced out the window where wind buffeted the passing trees. The train seemed to be moving at a decent clip. The rain continued, no doubt making a few leaf buds happy.

"I'm glad you woke up. I've been anxious to tell you something." An animated edge heightened Rolf's voice to a squeaky pitch. "While you were sleeping, I got up to go to the restroom in the back of the car. But the door was locked, so I moved on to the next car. As I came to the restroom door, a big Russian soldier was exiting, swinging his duffle bag out into the aisle. The bag banged right into me. I couldn't help noting the name tag—Ivan Petrov."

Rolf shook his short bangs away from his forehead. "The soldier looked at me and made direct eye contact without even an 'excuse me.' Something about his face… I'd seen him before. And it took me only seconds to remember."

Rolf's voice went higher as his words tumbled out faster. "He's the one we had a run-in with on our way to Anna's. And then before that, come to think of it, he had one with Liddy while I was in the breadline at the bakery a while back."

"Really? The guy's been everywhere." Marek sneered and pressed his lips flat. "Tell me about the one with Liddy? Can you recall?"

"Back then, I was too far away to hear what they were talking about. But I could see enough to know that Liddy was pretty mad."

Marek gritted his teeth. His fists clenched and unclenched repeatedly. "Wouldn't you know. This confirms what I suspected before—we've got two fellows in search of the same girl. He's following me. Now the question is—will I get there in time to be the first? Who knows? I may need your help to create a diversion."

He looked over to a fellow passenger across the aisle. "Excuse me. Do you think we're still on time?"

"According to my calculations, we've lost about twenty minutes, taking into account when we were supposed to leave the last town."

"Not good news." Marek pulled out a newspaper to keep his mind off the schedule.

Time went slowly, and about an hour later, the train slowed dramatically.

"Are we at the next stop?" Marek lifted in his seat, craning for a view out the window.

"No, no. This is unexpected." The fellow passenger across the aisle fidgeted, his brow wrinkling. Loud noises of clashing metal and sparks erupted underneath the car. "That did not sound good!"

The car shuddered to a complete stop.

"What's happened?" Marek eased from his seat, squeezing in between Rolf and the seat before them for a clear look out the window.

"Must have problems with the track underneath," the man nearby yelled.

Rolf stroked his eyebrow.

"Don't tell me that." Marek gasped, pressing his face against the window for a better view.

Other passengers rose to their feet. A conductor soon made his way through the car, announcing there would be a delay due to track failure.

"How long do you think?" Marek yelled back at him, his eyes wide.

"Might be several hours. We've got to get a track repair crew out here."

Marek turned toward Rolf. "It's not looking too good."

"I didn't want to say anything," the boy replied.

"Here. May as well bide your time munching on this apple." Marek reached with it toward Rolf, who snatched it out of his hand so quickly, it must have been pent-up energy.

Marek slumped in his seat, stared at his wristwatch, and then leaned to his fellow passenger nearby. "What's your best guess?"

"It all depends on when that crew gets here and how bad we're derailed. It was probably caused by washout from days of heavy rains. I wouldn't put my money on anything sooner than Munich by midnight."

Munich by midnight. I can probably live with that, but not a minute more. Sounded like the name of some new song. It had better be short and have a happy ending.

Several hours later, Marek found himself pacing the aisle. Sitting in his seat, when he desperately needed the train to be moving, tortured him, so he walked twelve paces to the end, turned, then came back again, as if he could somehow reach Munich. His head was now starting to throb. That, on top of a growling stomach not satisfied by the apple and crackers he'd brought, combined to sabotage any hopes for a reunion with Liddy. The crew had only recently arrived, and he was beginning to fear Munich by midnight was a stretch.

Well into the evening, the conductor strolled into the car. Marek dropped a magazine to his lap and focused on the man's lips. Would he have an update? The conductor strode midway down the aisle and asked everyone for their attention.

"I would like to give you the latest, folks. We have just spoken with the crew. I'm sorry to report that additional equipment will be needed to get the locomotive wheels back on the rails. Unfortunately, that equipment will not be here until early in the morning. We're extremely sorry for this delay."

Marek's fist smashed his few remaining crackers. *I'll miss connecting with Liddy. Why, Lord? Why? Why do You do this to me?* He rapped his hand several times against the train's side panel. *I'm desperate for Your help, Lord!*

At least the following morning brought sunshine, in addition to the long-awaited equipment. But thinking about his missed opportunity to connect with Liddy, Marek wondered whether God just plain didn't want it to happen. Did he not love her enough? He so longed to see her, to embrace her, but obstacles kept getting in the way. Maybe this was God's way of telling him to move on.

Then he remembered. Maybe the trip to Munich wouldn't be a total waste. He reached into his back pocket for the note he'd made a point to save—the one from the other young woman.

A loud noise from outside on the opposite side of the train interrupted his thoughts.

Chapter 14

Marek had heard the sound the day before—the squeal of brakes trying to stop tons of metal in motion. Now the light coming through the side windows dimmed, as other windows flashed by, like frames from a motion picture film that had gone out of sync. They finally came to a complete stop, just a few feet away. Had a train heading in the opposite direction met a similar fate as his train? Some work crew must have decided to fix both sides of the track while they were at it. Concerned eyes from the train car on the other side stared back at him.

Marek didn't feel so alone. His disappointment in not making his destination was now being shared. Travelers destined for Berlin would not make their destination on time just as Munich had been denied to him. Life seemed fairer, although, still hugely disappointing.

The train car across from him teemed with men, women, and children of all ages. But why would so many want to go to Berlin, a city so ravaged by war?

Down at the end of the other car, a young lady stood up, her back to him. She lifted an infant above her head, playfully jostling him. The baby was crying, his face red and mouth wide open, no doubt letting his mother know the loud and sudden stop had scared him. Nearby passengers stared up at the child, irritated expressions contorting their faces. A few moved away from the young mother. The woman cradled the baby in her arms, swaying from side to side. And now she turned around.

Marek gasped. *Could it be? This woman looked like Liddy! Oh, sweet Liddy. Is that really you? But... with a baby?* He must get on that train. *First, off this one. Please, trains, stay where you are—don't move quite yet.*

"Look, Rolf! I think I see Liddy on that train."

The boy's head swiveled like on a spring.

"My gosh. You just may be right!" He stood in disbelief.

"I've got to go over. Watch my things, will you?" He darted down the long aisle toward the door, forced it open, and leapt off the car. His foot slid as it hit the wet gravel, bringing him to one knee. Something sharp gouged through his trouser leg. Ignoring it, he stood up and looked down the track at the links of cars stretching out in both directions.

Which way was the shortest? Too many cars each way—no choice but to go underneath. But might the other train start up again?

He flopped onto his belly, the rough rocks of the track bed underneath stinging, then began to crawl, his heart beating rapidly. Condensation dripped off rusty mechanicals, and the smell of oil burned his senses.

Stay away from those wheels. Under one train car, now the other.

A loud noise sounded, and he flinched as the other car lurched forward a foot. *Had to be a final positioning of the train before work was to be done. It'd better be.*

He crawled a few feet more. Then, full daylight. He sprang to his feet and brushed off his clothes. He ignored a red spot seeping through his pants. After jumping up the steps and through the other train car's entry door, he stormed down the aisle, knocking over a small child, then helping him back up.

"Liddy, Liddy, it's me!" He rushed toward her.

She turned to him, eyes startled. First, a quick deposit of the baby onto the seat, covering him, his head and all, with a blanket. Then she leapt into Marek's arms, her soft shoulders collapsing against him, now captive to his unrelenting squeeze, the gentle fragrance of her perfume tickling his nose, reminding him how long it had been since that last happened.

"Oh, Marek! Can this really be you?" Her tears flowed freely as he rocked her back and forth in his arms.

"God has answered my prayers. Praise God!" he exclaimed, his strokes of her silky hair as tender as his exclamation was strong.

"What a glorious day!" Liddy tilted her head back to stare into his eyes. She brushed the hair on his brow to the side, her delicate touch electric.

"Yes, yes, yes. I was on my way to find you." He peered down at the baby. "What are you doing with this little one?" His gaze lingered on the infant.

"Marek, he's mine, but... it wasn't my fault. I'm so sorry... so so sorry...."

Her chin dipped down, her eyes closed, and her cheeks flushed as she snuck a quick peek at the baby. Her tears of joy upon seeing Marek abounded. But now the pendulum of emotions seemed to swing the other way. She began sobbing as she buried her head against his chest.

"What happened, Liddy? What does this all mean?" He took a slow breath and felt the warmth of his cheeks flushing as a mounting uneasiness bubbled up, coming from deep within.

"Oh, Marek! It was a nightmare," Liddy started out slowly. "When they came barging into the bakery in the middle of the night, then..." She stopped short. "I just can't talk about it."

"It's okay, Liddy. It's okay." He pressed the words into her ear, breathing in a faint scent of cinnamon reminiscent of the bakery. *Was that just his imagination or wishful thinking?* After all, he knew full well that all was still not okay with him.

"But who came barging in?" he queried with probing eyes.

"Russian soldiers. And one of them felt emboldened... and he took liberties. It was horrible."

Marek grimaced, and his teeth gritted as he shook his head, disgust writhing through him. "Don't tell me any more! If only I could get my hands on that bloke..."

"But what does this mean, Marek?" Liddy's lips quivered.

"What are you getting at?"

"For us?" A loud sniffle followed. "Hush, now... shhh. Everything will sort itself out." He sensed her lingering embarrassment and wanted to move on from the awkward moment, turning his attention back to the world around them.

"You know what? I'm bound back to Berlin now, and the best part is it's with *you*! What are the chances our two cars would be stuck next to each other like this? So much has happened that we must share." He stopped short and raised his head. "Oh no. My things are still on that other train." He started to pull away. "Who knows when it will take off again?" He squeezed her hand to reassure her that he'd be right back, but it took more than a moment to settle the trembling. Tears seeped from the corners of her eyes, and he moved back closer.

"No, I can't leave you. After all that you've gone through, I'm staying right here, next to the one I've been yearning for all this time. "

Liddy's mouth widened with a quivering smile that somehow emerged, overcoming tear-soaked, puffy, red cheeks.

"Here, let's sit down." He reached to hold her hand tighter. "We still have a long trip back to Berlin. I know you've gone through a traumatic time. Try to relax, knowing the worst is behind you."

She proceeded to relate the incredible stories behind the birth of her child, the Russian father who continued to harass her, her father's death and mother's stroke, the bakery's burning down, and her meeting up with Keppler.

As Liddy spoke, Marek crossed his arms and turned his head away with a loud exhale. Heat flushed through his body as he thought about all the ordeals that she had suffered through. "You've had to endure so much. To think, all of that happened in just a year. Your parents are no longer a part of your life. But becoming a mother—that's got to be the biggest change." He peeked down at the little one, pulling his blanket down below his chin.

"It's been so stressful, Marek. I pray God will bring me some peace this year." They both sat in quiet reflection.

Then Marek broke the silence. "I, too, had my own nightmare when I was forced into a death march to the Baltic Sea." He told her about the bombing of the *Cap Arcona* and his trek back home to Warsaw to find his mother but no father. "Strange thing about the Russians, though. You've had a horrible experience with them. I think they saved my life." He also described his recent visit to see Liddy's mother. "Communication is indeed a struggle."

"I guess God has brought both of us through some unbelievable challenges." She looked at her reflection in the window glass and sighed. "I see that reflection and wonder how you were even able to recognize me."

"I would never forget your beautiful face. But what counts is the person inside. You know what Scripture says: 'For the righteous fall seven times and rise again.' "

"Amen." Her shoulders sloped, then stiffened, rising with her chin before she brushed her cheek against her baby's fine hair. "But I've been too weary to count what number we're at."

Marek smiled at the baby she snuggled. "What's his name?"

"I…" She hesitated. The confession came out softly as she bit her lower lip. "I haven't named him."

Marek jerked his head and shoulders back a bit. "Oh?"

"I was going to let the family who adopts him pick the name. Yesterday I was all set to hand him over. But then today I backed out."

"Ah, that explains everything. Your mother stressed the date and wrote 'Gone' on a piece of paper. I thought it meant you were going somewhere, and I'd never find you. But instead, she meant that the baby would be gone." He released a heavy sigh. "Now that I've found you, I'm worried this baby situation is pulling you down. So, I'd love to hear why you changed your mind about the adoption. But only if you feel like sharing with me."

"Well, I thought it was a good Christian family. I had gotten to know them pretty well. They were desperate for a child. But in the end, I found out they had lied to me about their own well-being and ability to raise him."

"Was that the only reason?" He tipped his head and glanced sideways at her.

"Well, no, there is another reason. Physically handing him over to someone would have been so difficult. Another reason I didn't give him a cute name. My heart wasn't ready yet." She turned away, her voice fading.

"I can only imagine." He gazed down.

"He's my own flesh and blood, Marek." Her chin trembled, her soft lips parting as though a shiver had traversed down her spine.

"I understand." He reached to hold her hand, and their eyes met, remaining fixed. "What are you going to do now?"

"I don't know." She drew in a breath and rubbed the back of her neck. "Perhaps there's some other family out there I could get comfortable with. Now, at least, I have a chance to go show him to Mother. She hasn't seen her grandson yet." She paused to reflect, gazing out the window, then turned to him. "While there, I also want to try to convince her to make a move to Munich. I found a much better place for her. And of course, she'd be closer to family. Munich is also under American control, which I expect will be better for all of us."

"There's a lot to sort out, no doubt about that." Marek nodded curtly.

The baby stirred. Liddy stood up to rock him. Cuddling him, she twisted to her left, facing the window of the train car now directly opposite her. "I can't believe it! There he is—walking through your car headed to Munich. That's Ivan." Her visage turned white.

"How do you know Ivan?" Marek stood to glimpse as well.

"Ivan is the Russian soldier—the father!" She clenched her jaw as the color returned to her face.

Chapter 15

Marek clamped an arm around Liddy's shoulder and glared out the window. The man appeared to be lost in his own world, oblivious to the scowl now forming on Marek's face. "I ran into that guy earlier by the burned-out bakery. An ugly moment for sure."

"Need I say *all* my encounters with him have been ugly?" Liddy exclaimed, her mouth sneering and nostrils flaring.

"I feel like going over there to separate a few limbs from that body. I don't care how big he is." Marek shook his head. "But I dare not risk losing you. He's been following me, thinking I would lead him to you."

She turned her huge blue eyes on him. "But how is it… that he knows you?"

"He's the one who's been spying on Anna's apartment where I've been staying."

"Oh, that's right. I remember I flashed him a picture of you once." She pulled the picture with ragged corners from her pocket. "Well, he'll be surprised to find neither you nor me when he gets to Munich."

"Major surprise! And if they can get this train going soon, we'll be celebrating our reunion together tonight in Berlin." Marek took a deep breath, savoring the moment as they found their seats again. For the next forty-five minutes, they sat reflecting on all that had just happened. When he stared over with joy at the baby in Liddy's arms, he stroked his fingers for the first time across the infant's forehead. "Such a cute child of God."

While they were talking, the whistle on the southbound steam engine sounded off, indicating an imminent resumption of the trip to Munich. "Guess they've finally gotten that one ready to go. They should be able to devote full attention to this one now. I'm so anxious for us to get back to Berlin."

"By the way, on that other train there was a wonderful young fellow I was traveling with—he was trying to meet up with relatives in Munich. Anyway, too late to retrieve my belongings. I'd forgo them any day, though, in exchange for you. And of course this little guy." He reached over and grabbed his tiny foot. "But then he does need a name."

"Say," Marek continued. "I was just thinking...." He thrust his fist to the sky. "I've got a great idea. Why don't you name him Klaus after your father?"

"You must be kidding!" Liddy jolted toward him. "Think about it, Marek. A Russian killed my father. Another Russian violated me. My father would be weeping in heaven knowing that the offspring of a Russian bears his name."

"Look at it this way, Liddy. We know God loves this child unconditionally. The child's history and heritage have nothing to do with anything. If your father were still here, he'd love his grandson just as God does, with Christ-like, *agape* love. That's your father's legacy."

Liddy's brow furrowed as she pressed her lips together. Finally, she nodded. "You know… you're right. I think he would."

"And the love you have for your child will grow." He nodded with a smile. "And match the love you have for your father."

"I've been praying so hard about all of it, Marek. I've been so traumatized ever since that night. It's just taken my heart awhile."

"Well, only you went through it all, not I. It's easy for me to say. But I think you should name him Klaus in honor of your father."

She squeezed her little bundle tight and gazed into his eyes. "Yes, I'm going to do that. I think Mother will be happy, too, once she sees him. But here, since it was your idea, why don't you be the first to hold the little boy named Klaus?" She eased the baby into Marek's welcoming arms.

For several moments, his gaze was transfixed on Klaus's peaceful blue eyes.

"I wonder, though," Liddy pondered. "Won't it now be that much harder for me to give him away if I've named him Klaus?"

Marek did not answer but sat in thought. *Could I love this child the way he deserves? I would expect so! Will I always think of the real father when I see him? Probably at first, yes.* He looked down at the infant sleeping in his arms, his blanket rising gently with each breath.

But I won't think about the real father after a while, no! Will I be thrilled when he takes his first step or throws his first ball? Without a doubt. But what about me? Have I been through so much that I'm damaged goods? Being a father is no simple task! All his thoughts kept swirling around. He asked God for help to sort them out.

"Oh… say…" Marek finally continued, facing Liddy directly. "There's another, even more important part to my great idea. I know we've both been through so much this past year. But all said and done, I have to believe that God was only toughening us up for what was to follow." He handed the baby back over to Liddy and cleared his voice. "I don't know if I am even worthy, but I would be extremely happy to raise him with you as Klaus's father."

"What? What are you saying, Marek?"

"I'm asking you if you'll marry me, Liddy."

"Yes! Yes!" She flung an arm up and beamed. "Can it be this moment has finally come?"

"Being away from you for so long has been the worst part of my whole ordeal. My love for you has only gotten stronger. I love you more than you can ever imagine."

A radiant glow now swathed her face as she looked upward. "Oh, thank You, my dear God," Liddy shouted out, her eyes wide. "I can't believe this is happening. Are you sure you want me with all my history? You've been fretting over your own. Mine is still real and most definitely alive...." She chuckled. "But then it does come with a cute smile!" Her eyes sought to lock on Marek's. "Do you mean it?"

"Yes, without a doubt. We *all* are made for one another." His voice cracked with emotion. "But you'll have to forgive me," he went on. "Between the two trains stalling, I didn't have the opportunity to get out and buy a ring."

She laughed, then gazed dreamily into his eyes. "I would love nothing more than to marry you."

They shared a long kiss. A whistle blew, and the train lurched forward, moving on its way to Berlin.

Marek was about to check the progress outside when a familiar voice from the aisle started him. "Sir, I believe this belongs to you."

"Oh, Rolf! What are you doing here? This can't be. And with my suitcase? Thank you! But now you've missed your train to Munich."

"That's all right." The boy shrugged, a goofy grin quirking his lips. "I never wanted to go there in the first place. Especially without you. I also have your rucksack back at the other end of the car." With a jerk of his thumb, he pointed back. "Too hard to get both of them through the aisle before finding you."

"No problem—at least it's on this train. I'm amazed you were able to get as far as you did. Well now, here, sit down. You remember Liddy, right?"

"Oh, sure. Hi, Liddy." He cast her an admiring smile, which she reflected right back at him.

"Of course, I know Rolf," Liddy interjected. "He used to play with Willy. They shared a lot of grand times together. That brother of mine, by the way, is back in Munich with his grandparents."

"So, Rolf." Marek braced an arm around the boy's shoulders. "Let me introduce you to this little guy named Klaus. Liddy and I have just decided to get married." That final word had a most magical ring to it.

"Really?" Rolf's mouth fell open.

"And there's some other things going on which I'll get to, but I'll ask first if you'll go retrieve my rucksack. Will you please?"

"No problem." The boy bustled off.

"Liddy," Marek said in a soft voice as he leaned closer, "I have some sad news. Rolf has lost both his parents."

"No!" Her head jerked back, followed by a heavy sigh. "Oh my goodness. I can relate to that kind of loss, but as a youngster, it has to be so much more difficult."

"Well then, sweetheart," Marek continued. "Hear me out. Since you've surprised me with your little one, I'd like to surprise you in turn. Our family of three needs rounding up to four. Let's add Rolf. What do you say?"

After some quiet thought, Liddy replied, "Say, I think you've got a great idea, Marek. We can make it work. Let's do it! But don't forget there's Willy, now with his Oma. With him that makes five."

As Rolf returned, Marek couldn't wait to yell out, "Welcome."

Puzzlement squinched the boy's face. "What's that for?"

"Welcome to the family." Marek slapped him on the back. "We hope you'll join us."

"Really?" Rolf gasped, his eyes bulging as he looked back and forth between Liddy and Marek. "You mean actually be a part of the family? I can't believe this!" He let out a deep, satisfied breath. "I was worried about what I'd do." A wide smile now commandeered his face, and it appeared it would be plastered there all the while for the long trip back to Berlin.

"We're not done." Marek chuckled. "There's another reason. You see, I want to bring my father's compass back into the family."

"What?" Liddy asked.

"I found it in the street by the bakery," Rolf was quick to add. He pulled it out of his pocket.

"So that's what happened," Liddy replied. "I've fretted over losing it. I must have dropped it on my way out. Well, by all means, I'm happy it's now returned as a part of the family."

A jolt of movement by the train car signaled the long-awaited departure. Marek looked out the window in disbelief over all that had just happened. A broad smile stretched his face. As the train inched ahead, he could not help but notice two men giving each other congratulatory slaps on the back. Then he did a double take. "My, that man looked like Herr Keppler." He jerked his head farther, trying to get a better view of the faces soon fading into the distance.

"Really?" Liddy stretched her head around trying to get a view, as well. "I didn't see." She slapped her hand to her knee and frowned, then pressed both palms to her cheeks. "But it could have been. When I saw him in the POW camp, he mentioned rail repair." Her frown disappeared as an all-knowing smile spread across her face.

Marek tilted his head toward her and nodded. "Maybe he's the one who decided the rail on this side should be fixed at the same time. Strange coincidence, but fortunate, indeed." He put his arm around Liddy and grinned, overjoyed that he finally had the one he loved in his grasp, a promising family in tow, and that Ivan was on his way to find no one in Munich. Its whistle blaring once again, the train moved faster, getting up to speed, carrying the four of them toward their future together.

The End

Author Notes

My primary source for depicting post WW II Germany was the book: *Germany 1945* by Richard Bessel (New York, NY, Harper Collins, 2010). In it you'll find more detail about actual historical events such as the death march to the sea, the bombing of the *Cap Arcona*, the Russian invasion and treatment of women, and the activities of the Prisoners of War (POW's), such as railroad track repair and graveyard duties.

Lilias Trotter was a missionary to Algeria in the late 1800's. See the website under her name. The hymn, *Be Still My Soul*, in the public domain, was published in 1752 by Katharina A. von Schlegel.

www.ingramcontent.com/pod-product-compliance
Lightning Source LLC
LaVergne TN
LVHW011708060526
838200LV00051B/2811